BLURRED LINE

A NOVEL

**A
ROBERT LANE
NOVEL**

*To Evelyn
Bestwishes
Robert Lane*

About the Author: Robert, and his wife Kim, have been married for 34 years, and reside in the beautiful Okanagan Valley, located in British Columbia, Canada. They have two adult sons, and four grandchildren.
  Robert has been a Ranch hand, Logger, and Millworker. He has enjoyed reading books from the time he was very young.

BLURRED LINE by Robert Lane
Copyright 2016 by Robert Lane

ISBN 10 -1523997664
ISBN 13- 978-1523997664

PROLOUGE

Detective Mike Chance was lying in bed, staring at the ceiling, enjoying the last few minutes of relaxation, before arising and allowing the world with all its trials and tribulations intrude into his life. Hearing the hinges on the bedroom door emit its usual tiny squeak of protest at having to work, Mike was ready to tell his wife he's up, but chokes back the words when he hears two little girls giggling and telling each other to be quiet or daddy will wake up. Closing his eyes and feigning a deep sleep, Mike was unable to control the wide grin on his face as he listened to his favorite munchkins sneak up on him. Feeling their presence at the side of the bed he was still taken by surprise when they both launched themselves and land on him, simultaneously yelling. "Wake up daddy!" Laughing with joy and unabashed love for his two daughters Mike puts a big arm around each girl and hugging them until they squeal with delight, he than tells them they almost scared him to death.

"So, what brings my two favorite munchkins in the world sneaking into my bedroom and almost scaring me to death," asked Mike.

"Mommy said to come and wake you," four-year-old Desiree explained, snuggling closer to her dad.

"Well I think we should declare today a snow day and we all stay home," declared Mike

"Oh, Daddy you're so silly," exclaimed six-year-old Alicia.

Looking at his oldest daughter with a look of pure innocence Mike asks her why is he silly.

"It never snows in Metro-City," she responds in her most serious voice.

PROLOUGE

"Well then girls, I guess we had better get up and at her, if Alicia says it never snows here then I guess we can't have a
snow day. Go tell Mommy I'm up and we will have breakfast together." Feeling the girls weight leave the bed Mike was surprised when he thought he heard his girls calling Daddy from a long distance away.

   Jesus Christ! I can't believe that was a dream, with his eyes now wide open, Mike was sure he still felt the weight of the girls on his arms, the heat from their bodies on the rumpled sheets, as well as the sound of their laughter reverberating within his ears.

CHAPTER ONE

As ordered by his boss Sergeant Gwyn O'Mallory, Patrolman Mike Chance entered squad room 1 at precisely 07:45. He's surprised to see that the room is already three quarters full with members of the 08:00 to 1600 shift. Spotting an empty chair in the back row he quickly makes his way to it. Seating himself, he looked around at the assembled cops wondering what this early morning meeting is about.

Hearing the door open Mike turns his head and grimaced his boss, the repugnant Sergeant O'Mallory enter the room. Mike was barely able to repress a look of disgust as he witnessed the sweating, diminutive, over weight Sergeant laboriously make his way to the podium, situated in the middle of the dais at the head of the room. The Sergeant has gone out of his way to make Mike's rookie year as a patrolman as tough as possible. Using his position of authority to embarrass Mike at every opportunity. When Mike confronted him about this O'Mallory wearing a smirk that Mike would have loved to erase, refuted any such claims and advised Mike to just do his job.

Mike had asked Randy Wilson, the veteran patrolman that he has been placed with for his rookie year about this harassment. Randy explained. "Ya he's an asshole alright. The stupid son of a bitch tried three times to make Detective, and word has it he failed miserably each time. So, the Police Department in their infinite wisdom thought they should reward failure, and make him desk sergeant."

"Well how the fuck does he pass the annual physical?" queried Mike.

BLURRED LINE

"Exercise a small degree of discretion Mike" warned Randy.
"O'Mallory is unfortunately your senior officer and given his
mean streak would love to have you up on insubordination
charges."
Staring at Randy, Mike reiterates his question. "Don't be naive
Mike," groaned a tolerant Randy.
"Think about it, if the Department is stupid enough to make him
Sergeant do you really think he is going to fail his physical?"
Having finally gained the podium Sergeant O'Mallory surveys
the room with a pair of small pig like eyes, while catching his
breath. Using the palm of his fat hand as a gavel, he smacked the
top of the podium with enough power to closely imitate a clap of
thunder. Seeing that he has now captured the attention of the
room, he begins to speak in a voice roughened by many years of
tobacco use. "Okay, we have some business to take care of this
morning. We have two rookies, Mike Chance and Larry
Donovan who have now completed their mandatory year riding
with a veteran." This statement was met with the obligatory
smattering of polite applause from the assembled men and
women. "The Department has asked me to convey their gratitude
to Randy Wilson and Blake Guenther for their patience and
guidance in working with these rookies. Since Randy and Blake
have requested to partner up again, I now have to find partners
for Mike and Larry." Glaring balefully at the crowd O" Mallory
asks. "Is there anyone here stupid enough to want to change
partners?" Not seeing any hands rise into the air, O'Mallory
grins and states. "That's good saves me a bunch of fuckin
paperwork. okay we're done here. Larry and Mike stay seated,
everyone else get the hell out," concluded "Well, what the hell
are you two waiting for? A written invitation," barked
O'Mallory. "Get your asses up here." As Larry and Mike
approach the Sergeant it becomes clear to them that O'Mallory is
not about to relinquish the height advantage afforded by the dais,
and will remain there forcing them to look up at him.

BLURRED LINE

"Do you two know each other?" growled O'Mallory. Pointing at Mike, Larry answers "Seen him around."

Mike at six feet three inches and two hundred and thirty-five pounds felt small standing next to Larry, who is six feet six and weighs two hundred and seventy pounds.

"Hi there my name is Mike Chance," was Mike's innocuous greeting.

Extending a hand, the size of a baseball glove Larry responds simply with "Larry Donovan."

Fearing for the safe return of his hand Mike tentatively shakes the proffered hand. Observing Larry's gray hair and glacial blue eyes Mike can't help but comment. "Sort of young to have gray hair."

"It's not gray, it's silver," Larry replied tersely.

Stifling a chortle Mike responded. "Silver? Never heard of people having silver hair, gray yes but not silver."

"My old man had silver hair and I have silver hair, do you have a problem with that?" growled the now irate Larry.

"No not at all Larry, if you want to call it silver then silver it is," Mike quickly agreed at the same time turning away to hide his grin. "Okay, Okay, enough I just wanted to introduce you two guys not stand here and listen to your fuckin life stories. Now that you have met each other consider yourselves partners for the next 6 months. The Department also requested that I congratulate you on your becoming full time members of the Police force, so congratulations," he finished with a sneer.

"Now get the hell out of here and don't make me look bad by screwing up out there."

As the two of them exit the squad room, Mike over hears Larry murmur. "What an asshole."

As the two partners locate their patrol car and head out to "Protect and Serve" the citizens of Metro-City, they guardedly begin to relate facts about themselves.

After an un-eventful four hours of police work, Mike feels his stomach begin to protest regarding the lack of nutrients, and suggests to Larry that eating would be a good thing.

BLURRED LINE

"Ya I here ya Mike. You ever been to the Mexican Place called Miguel's, it's over on third street?" asked Larry.

"Yes, I have, really like his Nachos, their loaded with Jalapenos," Mike smiled in anticipation of burning lips.

"Si Senor," stated Larry returning the smile.

Pushing through the Bat-wing style doors into Miguel's, Larry and Mike wait patiently to be seated. The popularity of the restaurant and its spicy food, is borne out by the number of patrons seated at the tables, placed a discreet distance from each other. The open kitchen facing the seated customers, allows them to watch the antics of the three chefs and their assistants.

Pushing back from the table and emitting an explosive belch, Larry groaned "Jesus, I'm going to have to have a nap now."

Using the napkin to remove the last vestige of hot sauce from his burning lips, Mike wholeheartedly agreed.

Looking at his watch and seeing that their break was just about over Mike catches their waiters eye and asks for the check.

Approaching the table their waiter informs Mike that the meal is on the house.

Reading the name tag pinned to shirt of the waiter identifying him as Tyrone, Mike explained. "We just had a great lunch and now we would like to pay for it, so could you please bring us the check so we can pay up and leave."

"None of the other cops ever pay sir," stammered the uncomfortable Tyrone.

"Well maybe get your manager then and we will discuss it with him," suggested Mike

As Tyrone turned and walked away to locate his boss, Larry having quietly watched this by-play spoke up. "What the hell are you doing?"

"Well looks like I'm trying to pay for the meal," Mike answered dryly.

"Why?" He said all the cops eat here free."

BLURRED LINE

"That may apply to all the other cops, but it's not the way I do things." Mike replied brusquely.

Seeing the manager closing in on their table Larry waves him off, and continued. "What the fuck Mike, they offer a free meal you take it. In this world, there are wolves and there are sheep, the wolves take what they can, and we all know what happens to sheep, they gather into a flock and follow each other off the cliff," declared Larry with an irritating smirk.

Placing his forearms on the table, Mike leaned towards Larry arguing. "So, Larry, if you don't pay for the meal who does? Does the owner of the business deduct it from the wages of the manager and the waiter?"

Shrugging his shoulders Larry nonchalantly replied. "No concern of mine."

Waving the manager over, Mike asked him what happens when a customer does not pay for a meal.

"The owner deducts the price of the meal from my wages," he replied, stifling the beginnings of a smile.

Patrons seated at nearby tables, have become aware of the unfolding drama between the two cops, and are watching with blatant curiosity.

Staring at the manager's name tag Larry enquired. "Are you Mexican?"

"Si Senor, from Guadalajara".

"What the hell kind of Mexican name is Arnold?" demanded Larry.

"Senor, my poor father did not like his father in-law, who wanted my name to include his. So alas my father named me Arnold to spite his father in-law."

The snort that Larry emitted upon hearing this, clearly underlined his dis-belief.

Asking Arnold what the bill was, he informed Mike that its six dollars and fifty cents.

BLURRED LINE

"Fair enough," replied Mike and pulling a ten-dollar bill out of his pants pocket hands it to the manager and adds "Make sure the waiter gets a tip."

"Si Senor, Mochas Gracias."

Mike decided to play one last card. "So, Larry, if as you say Wolves are takers, and Sheep flock together and fall off a cliff, if you refuse to pay like all the other cops, does that make you a Sheep or a Wolf?"

"Well I'm sure as fuck not paying," snorted Larry with disgust as he stood up from his chair.

Back in their patrol car and having advised Dispatch they were once again available for calls, and despite the warm air outside its chilly inside the vehicle.

Larry who's sitting in the passenger seat, looked over at Mike driving and broke the chilly silence. "So, are you a good Samaritan, out to save the world? You must know the world can't be saved, all we can do is take what we can, while we can."

Thinking about what Larry has said, Mike responded. "That's pretty cynical Larry. I realize that the world might not be salvageable; but if I can make a difference right here where I live then yes, that would make me a good Samaritan. Now I have a question for you. Why did you become a cop?"

"Seemed like a good idea at the time, now I'm not so sure," looking askance at Mike

With a small smile on his face Mike commented. "We will agree to disagree." The remainder of their shift was spent in relative harmony, attending to a couple of minor car accidents.

The next morning Mike was dumbfounded when he set eyes on Larry.

"What happened to your hair?" Mike exclaimed staring in disbelief at the glaringly white scalp.

"Shaved it all off."

"What the hell for?"

"I sure didn't want to spend everyday day in a car with you making cracks about my hair!" declared Larry.

BLURRED LINE

"Hey, can I rub it?" laughed Mike, adding "What did your wife say?"

"She said you would want to rub it," Larry responded dryly.

"That wife of yours is a smart lady," chuckled Mike.

After a couple of weeks Larry, and Mike, seem to have moved past their original dispute, and settled into a comfortable routine.

Larry watches with a combination of amusement, laced with derision as Mike continues to pay for meals. One Friday morning as their shift began, Larry asked Mike if he and his wife would like to come over to Larry and Maria's for a barbecue Saturday night. "Sounds good, I will check with Adele and let you know," replied Mike adding. "This way our wives get to know each other as well."

"Ya that's what Maria was thinking." Then snapping his fingers remembered to ask Mike. "Hey Maria wanted me to make sure your wife's not a vegetarian as we will be barbecuing steaks with a baked potato."

"Holy shit! you mean real steaks not some sort of unidentifiable meat that has been ground up."

Laughing uproariously Larry responds. "That's funny Mike, of course the steaks are real."

"Unfortunately, trying to pay off school debts, and Adele's career just beginning, our budget doesn't have a lot of room for steak, so I can personally guarantee that we will be there, and thanks for the invitation."

CHAPTER TWO

Entering their tiny three-bedroom apartment Friday evening, Mike heard his wife Adele talking to their one-year-old daughter Alicia in the kitchen. Sitting down at the table he watched as Adele spoon fed some sort of green mush into Alicia's waiting mouth. "What is that stuff? asked a puzzled Mike.

"According to the label on the jar, this disgusting looking stuff contains all the nutrients Alicia needs to be healthy." answered Adele. Gesturing at Alicia's open mouth awaiting the next spoonful adding "She really likes it."

"Apparently," answered Mike.

Totally engrossed in watching his wife feed their daughter, Mike realized how truly fortunate he is. His beautiful wife Adele, all of five feet three inches tall, with obsidian colored eyes, and raven black hair that cascades to the small of her back. Mike is so involved in watching the interaction between mother and daughter, he almost forgot about Larry's invitation.

"Oh, ya sweetie. Larry invited us over for a barbecue tomorrow afternoon. It would just be the four of us."

"Barbecue what?" Adele asked absently.

"Steak," announced a beaming Mike.

"Do mean a real steak? Not something that began as hamburger," asked a now very interested Adele.

Outright laughing now, Mike confirmed that it will be a real steak.

"I'm sure my sister Roxie will look after Alicia for us."

On their way, over to Larry and Maria's Saturday afternoon, Adele asked Mike to once again describe Larry to her.

Thinking about it for a minute Mike begins. "He's a little loud. His laugh is very contagious.

BLURRED LINE

I believe he is loyal to his friends, but I have seen some glimpses of what might be called a vicious temper, I would not want him as an enemy."

As Mike turned onto the street where Larry and Maria live, he watched Adele absorb the quiet atmosphere of the neighborhood. The pristine Elm trees flourishing along the sidewalk, green grass growing on the boulevard, children playing jump rope in driveways.

"One day Adele, this is where we will be living," Mike promised.

Gazing across at her husband she replies with a simple "Yes."

"This must be the place," Mike commented as he parks the car alongside the curb in a cul de sac.

Exiting the vehicle Mike, and Adele begin walking up a short driveway, at the same time noticing the freshly cut lawn, with a border of sprouting multi-colored tulips. They both admire the moderately sized house, with twin Dormers projecting from the second floor, Mike was about to ring the doorbell when the door opened.

"Welcome, Welcome," boomed a smiling Larry.

Mike smothered a grin as he watched Adele visibly wince at the bombastic volume of Larry's voice.

Shaking Larry's proffered hand, Mike introduced him to Adele.

Mike chuckled as Larry in his exuberance, embraced Adele in a bear hug to the point where she almost disappeared.

"Come on in guys, don't worry about your shoes. We will join Maria on the patio," Larry bellowed in a slightly modified tone.

Moving through the interior of the house Mike and Adele take in the simple yet tasteful decor. Approaching the table and chairs situated on the patio in the backyard with a barbecue placed off to one side, Larry introduces them to his wife Maria. Mike and Adele were barely able to mask their surprise, when Maria stood up to find that she must be six feet in height.

BLURRED LINE

Displaying a warm smile, the statuesque lady with short auburn hair, soft brown eyes, and equally soft voice welcomed them, shaking Mikes hand and hugging Adele.

Seating themselves in the two un-occupied chairs at the table, Maria enquired if they would like a drink.

"Beer sounds good to me," replied Mike

"I would love a glass of Sparkling water if you have it," answered Adele.

"Coming right up," announced Larry jumping up from his chair to get the drinks.

After a few minutes of small talk Maria invites Adele on a tour of the house, taking their refreshments with them the two ladies who seem have a formed an instant rapport head inside.

The four adults have enjoyed an afternoon and evening of fine food, conversation and laughter. Adele and Mike have stated that when Mike's career in Law Enforcement, and Adele's career as a Tax Consultant are finally started they will want a home exactly like this one. As a highly-respected dancer in the local Ballet community Maria has invited Adele to her upcoming performance.

Regretfully at eleven p.m., Adele announced that they had better leave or else her sister who is minding Alicia, will think she has been abandoned. Saying their goodbyes Mike and Adele tell their new friends that evenings like this will now have to be a regular occurrence.

On the drive home Adele comments. "She glides."

"I'm sorry, who glides?" asked Mike.

"Maria, she doesn't walk, she glides," responded Adele

Thinking about this for a minute before replying Mike responded. "Well sweetie you glide too."

Smiling warmly at this circumspect reply, Adele informed him that his wise reply has earned him some valuable points him. With my short legs, I don't glide, but nice of you to say that."

15

BLURRED LINE

After a couple of minutes of silence Adele asked. "No comment?"

Smiling sagely Mike promptly countered with. "Hate to lose those points before I get a chance to redeem them."

Reaching over to rub her husband's shoulder she murmured. "I think the redemption department may be open tonight."

Parking the car in the underground parking lot of their apartment building, Mike asked Adele if she was going to use the elevator to their third-floor apartment.

Laughing she responded. "No I think I will just glide up the stairs as usual."

Sunday morning, Mike, wearing just his favorite ripped pair of sweat pants joined Adele and Alicia who were already in the kitchen. Pouring a cup of fresh coffee into a mug he asked Adele if she would like some.

"No thanks Michael I have a tea."

Leaning against the counter, Mike inhaled the heady aroma of the freshly percolated coffee.

"Did Larry join the Police force the same time as you Michael?"

"I believe so," contemplating her question, "Why?"

"Well I can't help but wonder how they can afford such a nice place, and we can barely afford this," grimacing, she gazes around the minuscule kitchen.

"It must be the fact that Larry doesn't pay for lunches," Mike replied jokingly.

Looking at her husband, Adele asked for clarification. Mentally kicking himself for opening this door Mike explained about his unwillingness to accept free meals.

"So, you're saying that you pay for your meals, and Larry doesn't."

Noticing Adele's arched eyebrows and recognizing signs of mortal danger, Mike continued in a vain attempt to defuse the situation. "I feel that by accepting free meals I'm placed in an obligatory situation."

BLURRED LINE

Staring at her husband, with Alicia chatting away in a language that only one-year-old infants understand, Adele icily responds with "Please continue."

Becoming somewhat agitated at having to defend his decision Mike carried on with his explanation. Pointing at Adele he began. "If you receive an unexpected gift don't you feel the need to reciprocate in kind?"

Silently pondering this statement, she guardedly nods her head in agreement, sensing victory Mike began to let down his guard, but his hopes were soon dashed.

"Your analogy is right; your argument is wrong. It was explained to you that all cops accept this, so why are you spending money for meals, that we could be using to save for a down payment on a real house, and get out of this shitty apartment. Do you feel that paying makes you better than the rest of the other cops?" questioned Adele, taking a breath she continued. "No wait, I know the reason why. You think you are a White Knight that will rid the city of crime, you have always thought that only you will be able to save the world from itself. In the meantime, your wife and family live in a shitty apartment the size of a shoe box." With tears beginning to escape the confines of her eyes Adele shook her head in frustration.

Mike felt the cheeks on his face become prickly with the sudden infusion of hot blood, as he defended himself against this unwarranted attack. "Is that truly what you think, that I 'm out to save the world from itself, and care more about the citizens of this goddamn city then I do of my own family."

Bursting into tears Adele replies bitterly. "Yes, I do. But unfortunately, I also happen to love you and we are pregnant again."

As the realization of Adele's last words penetrate through Mike's anger he quickly moves to her side of the table and envelopes her in a hug.

BLURRED LINE

Gasping for air and attempting to push her husband away Adele exclaimed. "Okay Michael, I can't breathe."

  Releasing her Mike rocked back on his heels, staring at his wife declared. "This is incredible we're going to have another baby. Maybe Alicia will have a baby brother."

"Or sister" added the now smiling Adele.

CHAPTER THREE

As Larry, and Mike make their way to their patrol car on a blustery spring morning Larry commented. "Hey Buddy, Maria met Adele for lunch the other day, and said that Adele is almost ready to have that baby."

"Yes," Mike agreed adding. "She said she was feeling a little weird this morning so I won't be surprised to get a call."

Slapping his friend and partner on the shoulder Larry declared "You are one lucky son of a bitch."

A couple of hours later while patrolling the notoriously rough neighborhood around Jo's Bar and Grill, Larry suddenly barks out "Stop the car."

With the car still rolling, Larry's agile form burst from the car, parking and exiting the vehicle, all Mike saw was Larry's back as he hurtled down an alleyway. Attempting to match Larry's speed at the same time exercising caution, Mike soon heard Larry's booming voice.

"What the fuck are you doing?"

Coming up beside Larry, Mike observed the ravished, mal-nourished, well-known drug dealer Curly, standing beside a young boy who looked no older than twelve.

Pointing a finger at Curly, Larry again asks in a booming voice. "What the fuck are you doing with this kid?"

Staring at the ground, Curly made some unintelligible reply that neither Mike nor Larry could understand.

"You're not selling him something, are you?" demanded an enraged Larry.

"What do you think I am, a drug dealer?" replied Curly sullenly.

Taking a different tack Larry asked the kid. "What's your name?"

BLURRED LINE

"Germaine" stammered the kid

"Okay Germaine, did this sack of shit sell you something?"

Looking fearfully at Larry, Germaine responded. "My mom sent me down here to get something for her headache."

Advancing till his face was inches away from Curly's, Larry once again asked with barely controlled fury what he sold to Germaine.

Watching this unfold, Mike wondered what type of mother would send her twelve-year-old into the dangerous world of buying illicit drugs. Feeling his cell phone vibrate in his pocket Mike looks at the screen and sees its Adele and she has sent their baby code.

Barely able to restrain his excitement Mike attempted to interrupt Larry.

"Larry, Hey Larry, we gotta go."

With a huge hand crushing the thin malnourished shoulder of Curly, Larry turned to face Mike. "What was that Mike?"

Wearing an enormous smile, Mike waved his phone and explained it's Adele, and she's at the hospital.

"Alright buddy." looking back at Curly, Larry muttered. "Looks like I don't have time to deal with you asshole." Then without warning, slams a fist the size of a ham into the jaw of Curly who promptly dropped to the pavement unconscious.

Looking at Germaine Larry asked him. "Where do you live?" Staring at the bleeding unconscious form of Curly, lying on the pavement Germaine told Larry his address.

"Okay Germaine you get your ass home, and tell your mom that we will be paying her visit shortly."

"So, what are we going to do about him?" Mike asks gesturing at the motionless Curly.

"Him? Hell nothing," responded Larry.

"Shit Larry, you hit him so hard he might not wake up."

"Then I guess the world will be a better place," adding "He only got what he deserves."

BLURRED LINE

Still unconvinced that Curly was even alive, Mike eased over to him, crouching down he picked up one of Curly's hands.
"What are you doing? Going to hold his hand for him?" asked Larry with a loud guffaw.
Not looking at Larry, and placing two fingers on Curly's left wrist Mike was relieved when he felt a pulse.
Releasing the hand, he stood up and looking at Larry commented dryly. "Well at least he's still alive."
"Too fuckin bad."
Then with a huge smile directed at Mike, Larry boomed "Let's go have a baby."
With both men taking huge strides back to their patrol car Mike can't help but grin and remark to Larry. "You ever want to take a swing at me, remind me to duck."
Laughing out loud Larry agreed to this, growling. "Nobody better fuckin hurt a kid while I'm around."
Dropping Mike at the Hospital, and wishing him and Adele good luck, Larry promises to stop in after his shift is over.
"You're not coming in?" asked Mike.
"No, that asshole O'Mallory would roast my nuts for me."
Searching for Adele's room in the labyrinth of hallways was almost impossible, convinced that he was not about to find it, he asks the first person he met.
"Maternity?" "Yes, just continue the way you're going and you can't miss it," directed a harried looking doctor.
Walking into the room assigned to his wife, Mike was dismayed to see three other beds in the room, all bearing ladies in the same condition as Adele.
With a quizzical look at the other beds, Mike quietly asked Adele why she doesn't have a private room.
"Your insurance does not cover a private room, but don't worry Michael, this is just the warm up room, when the action really starts we go to the delivery room."
Four hours later, and with jangled nerves Mike is convinced that fathers should not be invited into delivery rooms.

BLURRED LINE

Although the doctor reassured Mike that the delivery was an easy one, he remained skeptical.

Standing in the nursery holding his daughter, Mike heard a tapping on the glass, looking up he noticed Larry watching, and giving Mike thumbs up. Releasing his daughter into the care of the nurse Mike makes his way to the door.

"Congratulations buddy!" exclaimed Larry. "Is everyone good?"

"Yea we're all good," confirmed the emotionally drained Mike.

"Jesus, you look like you need a drink," he remarked with a grin adding. "Maria will be here soon."

Moving closer to the glass to see the baby, Larry observed. "So, I see by the pink blanket it's a girl, what's her name?"

"We have named her Desiree Maria," responded a beaming Mike.

Still engrossed in observing the baby, Larry turned to stare at Mike uttering. "Seriously?"

"Seriously, Adele and I had already decided that if it were a girl this is the name we wanted."

Speechless Larry grabbed Mike's hand, shaking it vigorously announced. "Maria will be so honored."

"We would also like to ask you two to be her god-parents when she is baptized." Upon saying this Mike was surprised to watch Larry turn suddenly away, and once again face the glass of the nursery.

"We would be incredibly honored to be your daughter's god-parents Mike," murmured a somber Larry.

Both men turn to face the loud click of fast approaching heels on the linoleum floor.

With arms, outstretched Maria hugged Mike, congratulating him on the birth of their baby girl.

Smiling at his wife, Larry commented. "Hi there Maria."

Returning the smile Maria answered. "Yes, hello Larry," then "So what room is the lady of the hour in?"

BLURRED LINE

Pointing in the direction of the room and relaying the room number Mike enquired of Maria. "How did you know it was girl?

"You're such a dear Mike, it's a little thing called a text, and your wife says she has another surprise for me," calling over her shoulder as she made her way to the room.

"Tell you what buddy, seems like everything is under control here why don't we go get that drink?"

"That is exactly what the doctor prescribed," answered Mike.

Comfortably ensconced in a booth at a bar just steps away from the hospital, Mike watches tears of condensation slide down the chilled bottle of beer.

"Here's to Desiree Maria," Larry announced raising his glass in a toast.

"Here, Here," clicking Larry's glass with his bottle Mike completed the toast.

May I ask why you and Maria have not had kids?"

Staring into his drink, gently swirling the contents around in the glass, Larry answers with brutal honesty. "My mother was a drunk, she lived only for her next drink. She died when I was only eight, it was then I realized why she was a drunk. My dad was a fuckin monster, while my mom was alive he would beat the shit out of her. He was smart enough to hit her where the bruises wouldn't show." Still staring into his glass as though searching for answers Larry continued. "After my mom died, the old man decided that I would be his next punching bag, that was when I realized that my mom chose death over the living hell she was in. This carried on until I was eighteen, then one night he tried to once again beat the shit out of me. He will never beat the shit out of anybody else," concluded Larry.

"Jesus Christ," murmured a shocked Mike. "What became of him?"

Swallowing the rest of his drink in a single gulp. Larry answered coldly. "Don't know, when I was done with him I didn't give a fuck if he was dead or alive.

BLURRED LINE

I promised myself that as soon as I could afford it I was having a vasectomy, there was no way in hell I would ever be my father.

Staring Mike in the eye, Larry continued. "You know what was worse than the beatings. Even though everyone in South-Bend knew what my old man did, no one stopped him. I tried to tell people, even the fuckin cops and no one listened. That was when I realized it was up to me to stop it as no one else gave a shit. I have nothing but contempt for people in authority, and have learned to trust only myself."

Absorbing all this information has shocked Mike, catching the bartenders eye indicated they would like another round.

"What has Maria said about all this?"

"She's okay with it, she accepts the fact that married to me there will be no kids, she jokes that pregnant ballerinas don't get many opportunities to dance. Therefore, you guys naming your daughter after her will mean the world to her."

Still stunned by this revelation of Larry's childhood Mike, at a loss for words murmured. "Jesus Christ."

CHAPTER FOUR

"Hey buddy you ever think about doing something different?" asked Mike while at the same time attempting to stifle a yawn.

"Like what, sleeping?" Larry replied with a grin as he looks away briefly from driving to observe the exhausted Mike.

"Ya not getting much of that these days, it seems that since Desiree has turned two, she wants to play all night rather than sleep. I have also been studying for the detective's exam as well as playing basketball at Jefferson High School with some teenagers. Funny thing one of the kids is the waiter from Miguel's, he still remembers that day we argued in there."

"Seems like a long time ago. So, what's this about the detective exam?" queried Larry.

"Adele has been putting on the pressure about a bigger place, she wants a house in the suburbs, and with what I make as a patrolman that's not going to happen. I began considering becoming a detective, I made the mistake of asking Sergeant O'Mallory about it and he went ballistic. Then I remembered that he had failed the exam three times, so I went over his head to the Chief of Detectives."

"And?" prompted Larry, curious about where this was headed.

"They advised me that they will have two people retiring in the next six months, so if I was interested this would be the time to take the exam."

"What the Hell, ya if you're going to do it then I might as well to, sure as fuck don't want to spend all day riding around with some new guy. I'm curious, what type of house is Adele looking for?"

BLURRED LINE

Chuckling, Mike answered. "Something like yours, she has loved it from the first time we were there. She has always asked how come we can't afford it, when you guys can."

Mike suddenly felt the painful bite of the seat belt digging into his shoulder as the car came to a tire screeching halt.

Looking over the hood of the car, in a vain attempt to ascertain why Larry had abruptly stopped the car, he was taken aback when he heard Larry speak in a low menacing tone.

"Don't go there Mike," growled Larry. "Don't ever ask that question, it's none of your fuckin business how I can afford it. We might be friends as well as partners in this fuckin car, but don't ever ask me that question!"

Mike was shocked, both at the heat in Larry's voice as well as the glacial cold emanating from Larry's ice chip blue eyes.

"Fuck you!" responded an equally pissed off Mike. "I don't give a flying fuck how you afford it. All I'm saying is my wife is giving me a fuckin hard time about a house, so fuck you asshole."

The rest of the shift was spent in an uncomfortable silence, in the locker room after changing back into their civilian clothes, Larry attempted to make amends. Slamming his locker door closed, Mike glared at Larry, then left without saying a word.

CHAPTER FIVE

As Mike surveyed his new desk in the detective division, he noticed the retiring Detective, Peter Lumpkin approaching. Sticking out his hand Peter congratulated Mike on his success, shaking the proffered hand, Mike thanked him, and wished him a great retirement. Spotting a manila folder in Peter's other hand, Mike pointed at it.

Seeming to have forgotten about it, Peter handed it to Mike saying. "Here, this is a file on the Delveccio brothers, they appeared on the scene about five years ago. It seems they are involved in all kinds of low life shit, everything from murder to extortion. I have had charges brought against them several times, but each time either the witnesses or the evidence seems to disappear. I am beginning to think they have protection within the Precinct," he concluded with a frown.

Sitting down at the desk, Mike opened the file and introduced himself to the Delveccio brothers.

As Larry sat down at his desk that is co-joined with Mike's, he asked. "Hey I thought you guys were coming over Saturday night. Maria was disappointed when Adele called and said that Alicia was unwell, hope she's feeling better."

"Ya she is, thanks for asking," responded Mike, not bothering to look up from the file he's absorbed in.

"What's that you're reading?" enquired Larry.

Still not looking at Larry, Mike advised him it's a file Peter Lumpkin gave him about two brothers he has been trying put away.

"Oh ya, you want to share it?

BLURRED LINE

Finally looking up, Mike reluctantly handed the thick file over to Larry. As Larry began to thumb through the file, Mike thought about how their friendship had changed since that episode in the patrol car.

Although they were both successful at becoming Detectives and remain partners Mike is now hesitant to associate with Larry outside of work.

Smiling, Mike remembers the expression on O'Mallory's face when he told him that he had passed the Detective exam. As O'Mallory expostulated turning red in the face with his anger, Mike was beginning to think the man was about to have a coronary. The most satisfying part was when Mike could say to him. "You're not my boss anymore, so screw you O'Mallory." As Mike turned on his heel and walked away, O' Mallory continued with threats about what he would do to Mike.

Looking up from the file, Larry witnessing the smile asked Mike what's up. "Just thinking about O' Mallory."

"Ya what an asshole," throwing the file onto the desk Larry commented. "That's bullshit, thinking those two morons have some sort of connection in the Precinct. That Peter guy lacked the guts to do what it takes to put those scumbags away, and figured he would say that to cover his ass," then in a tone of admonishment advised Mike. "Don't get on your high horse and waste time trying to pin something on these guys. We have enough work to do," he concluded pointing at the stack of files residing on the corner of the co-joined desk.

Feeling resentment begin to simmer at what Larry had said, Mike decides it's time to set the record straight "Actually Larry, what I do on my own time is none of your concern," retrieving the file and waving it in the air", Mike continued in a tone that brooked no argument. "If I want to waste time chasing these guys, I will. I certainly don't need, nor want your approval.

BLURRED LINE

The way I see it we may be partners at work, but that's all,"
declared Mike, watching the gray haired lanky form of their new
boss approaching.

"Good Morning." announced Lieutenant Jim Nickolas as he
arrives at the desk shared by his new detectives. With his glasses
perched precariously on the end of what could be best described
as a patrician nose he continued "I would like to take this
opportunity to welcome you two to the Detective division."
Seemingly unaware of the tension between his new detectives
Jim rambled on, advising them that if they have any questions
just knock on his door.

"Well good luck boys." and with that he spun on his heel and
retreated to his enclave.

Despite the low level current of animosity that now seems to
exist between Mike and Larry, they excel in their new career.
Over the next two years they solve many cases, they even
receive a commendation from the Metro-city Police
Commissioner, after solving a rather onerous case that had
plagued the detective division for years.

CHAPTER SIX

Immersed in a thick file regarding a series of unsolved burglaries, Mike barely heard Larry ask what time he must pick up his girls. Another ten minutes went by before Mike responded.

"Why what's up?" he asks.

"What's up where?" Larry answered.

Shaking his head and smiling he reminded Larry "You asked me what time I was picking up the girls and I was wondering why."

"Oh right." consulting the time on his watch commented "I have to leave at two-thirty for an appointment."

Shaking his head at this simple answer, Mike continued to smile as he once again attempted to decipher the mystery of the unsolved burglaries.

Shortly thereafter Mike felt what could easily pass as a mild earthquake on the rector scale, as Larry heaved himself out of his chair, muttering "See you tomorrow," and left the office.

Giving himself plenty of time to arrive promptly at four pm to get his daughters, Mike pushed back from his desk at three-thirty, rising from his chair he headed towards the doorway. He only managed a few steps before he was ambushed by his boss, Lieutenant Jim Nickolas.

"Hey Mike how's that report coming?"

"Hi Lieutenant, I just about have it completed," responded Mike impatiently.

"I couldn't help but notice that Larry left early."

"Yes, he had an appointment," glancing at his watch, Mike advised Jim that he must leave to be on time for his girls.

Not bothering to respond, Jim turns and dismisses Mike with a wave over his shoulder.

BLURRED LINE

Glancing at his watch, Mike silently swore realizing that if
traffic is congested he will not arrive at the girl's caregiver by
four o'clock. Adele and Mike, were arguing on a regular basis
about the time he spends at work, and being late to get the girls
would not help his already weak case. Arriving at Ellen Jacoby's
home, who is the caregiver for Alisha and Desiree, Mike curses
realizing that he is twenty minutes late.

Knocking on the door Mike braces himself for the expected
whirlwinds called Alisha and Desiree, and was surprised when
greeted instead by the short rotund figure of Ellen Hunt.

"Oh, Hello Mike, did the girls forget something?"

Surprised by this question, Mike apologizes for being a bit late
to pick up the girls, and was disconcerted to see a look of alarm
flash across Ellen's face.

"The girls aren't here Mike, it was so nice out that we decided
to wait for you outside on the lawn. The phone rang in the house
and I went to answer it, when I came back out Alicia and Desiree
were gone, I just assumed you had picked them up," she
explained.

Feeling an overwhelming sense of dread, Mike barged past
Ellen and enters the home, calling out to his girls to end this
game of hide and seek right now before they get in trouble. Not
receiving any response from the empty house, Mike turned back
to Ellen, and in a voice completely devoid of any warmth asked
her "Where in the fuck are my girls?"

Now visibly concerned, Ellen pointed to the backyard, Mike
hoping against hope rushed around the house to the back. The
first thing that he's aware of is a dollhouse that is more than big
enough to house two mischievous girls. With relief washing
through every part of his being, he approached the doll house
and flinging open the door yells "Surprise." Once again, he was
met with overwhelming silence, agitated to the point of
desperation, Mike hoped that Adele was able to pick up the girls
and forgot to let him know.

BLURRED LINE

Taking out his cell phone he called his wife, trying in vain not to let the intense fear he is feeling communicate itself to her. "Hi sweetie, did you pick up the girls today?" he asked when she answers her phone.

"No I didn't Mike, you said you were going to as I'm still tied up here at the office. Why? Are you going to be late, you promised you would be on time?"

"The girls aren't here," whispered Mike.

"What do you mean the girls aren't there, Ellen knew you were going to be there at four pm."

"Ellen is here but the girls aren't." then he quickly related what had happened in a voice filled with despair.

As Adele became cognizant of what Mike was telling her, she screamed into her phone "Find our girls Michael I will be there in ten minutes."

Deciding on a course of action Mike called his boss Lieutenant Jim Nickolas, to advise him of the situation giving him the address of Ellen's house. Mike was instantly gratified to hear Jim state he will have O'Mallory dispatch six radio cars to that location. Hearing his phone ring, Mike answering it hears Jim's voice once again, advising Mike he has mobilized the Police Chopper. Jim then asked Mike for a description of the girls and what they are wearing.

"Oh shit," Mike groaned knowing full well he had left for the office before the girls were even up this morning. Describing the girls to Jim, and the approximate time they went missing, Mike informed Jim he will call his wife to see what they were wearing. Racing to the front of the house, Mike found a completely distraught Ellen sitting on the front step with her head buried in her hands.

"You need to tell me exactly what happened here," commanded Mike in a tone of voice carved from ice.

"At what time, did you take the girls outside?"

"At three-thirty," she sobbed.

"What time did the phone ring?"

BLURRED LINE

Slowly regaining her composure, she was able to answer the question.

"At three-forty."

"How long were you in the house?"

Closing her eyes as though to concentrate she replied.

"No more than ten minutes."

As Mike slowly reviewed the time line offered by Ellen, he was beginning to think that for the girls to disappear in such a short time frame, that perhaps this was a crime of opportunity not a targeted kidnapping.

Looking up as heard the screech of protest emitting from tires sliding on pavement, Mike was surprised to see the lanky form of his boss emerging from a car and striding towards him.

"Hey Mike any news?"

Seeing Mike's negative nod. Jim placed his hand on Mike's shoulder and stated unequivocally. "I'm not going to give you some bullshit story about don't worry. What I will do, is promise you that all the resources available to me will be deployed. We will leave no stone unturned, in our search. Now where in the fuck are those radio cars?" Jim asks clearly perplexed they were not already there.

Pulling his phone from his jacket he impatiently punches in a number. "O'Mallory" Jim barks into his phone. "This is Lieutenant Jim Nicolas where in the fuck are those patrol cars?" he demanded. "I don't care what you have going on right now. If I don't see their faces in front of me in five minutes, I will be charging you with insubordination." The now red in the face Lieutenant vehemently turned his phone off.

Taking a moment while he regained his composure, Jim than suggested to Mike. "While we're waiting for those other cars Mike, where is your caregiver I would like to speak to her."

"She's at the house, I will go get her."

Arriving with Ellen in tow Mike introduced her to Jim.

"Don't I know you?" asked Jim as he studied Ellen's face.

BLURRED LINE

"Uh, no I don't think so," answered Ellen.

Still staring at her Jim remarked. "Yes, I'm sure we've met at some time, it will come to me. So, is there anything that you may have forgotten to tell Mike?"

Just then the promised patrol cars rolled in, and Jim asked Ellen to wait while he organized the search.

As the patrolmen congregate around the Lieutenant, he began barking orders.

"I want two of you on each side of the street interviewing these neighbors, see if they heard anything. Or if they were aware of unaccounted for vehicles in this vicinity between approximately three and four pm today. The rest of you I want a grid search set up for a ten-block radius, I want every nook and cranny gone through with a fine-tooth comb."

Hearing the squeal of brakes, Mike saw his wife Adele, emerge from the vehicle almost before it had completely stopped.

Calling out her husband's name she rushed over to him, her fear for their daughter's safety clearly visible on her face.

Attempting to quell the dread he was feeling Mike attempted to reassure her with "We will find the two munchkins."

Seeing Ellen standing alone on the lawn awaiting the return of Jim, Adele dis-engaged herself from Mike and hurried towards her, at the same time screaming. "What did you do? What were you thinking? How could you leave the girls alone like that?"

With her head bowed before this onslaught from Adele, Ellen murmured softly. "I'm so sorry, I'm so sorry".

Adele continued her barrage in a voice loaded with accusation and condemnation. "Sorry doesn't begin to cut it Ellen!" Waving her arm to encompass the yard she yells. "You left our girls alone in an unprotected yard, exposed to who knows what kind of human predator? What could have possibly been more important than our two girls?"

BLURRED LINE

Lifting her head and taking a long slow breath, Ellen slowly re-iterated what had transpired. Adele looked like she was ready to unleash another torrent of anger when Ellen admitted that she had showed poor judgment in leaving the girls.

"That is the world's greatest understatement Ellen! Do you not have voice mail to take calls when you are out?" Adele asked coldly.

Moving away from the two women, Mike punched in a number on his phone and when it was answered by his wife's closest friend Maria, quickly explained the situation. Then giving her the address asks her if she could possibly come to lend moral support to Adele.

"Of course, Mike, I'm already heading out the door I should be there shortly."

Mike than called Larry to inform him of what has occurred, but the call goes to his voice mail. Kicking the ground in frustration, and feeling completely forlorn, Mike was unable to prevent himself from thinking about what his girls might be going through.

Returning to Adele and Ellen, Mike informed Adele that Maria was on the way, and was unprepared for the look in his wife's eyes.

Staring accusingly at her husband with sparks shooting from her eyes, Adele informed Mike that Ellen had told her that he had been late again picking up the girls.

"I was held up at work, I was only twenty minutes late," he explained.

"Where are my girls Michael?" Adele demanded. "You couldn't even manage to get here on time to pick them up."

Recognizing the signs of battle in Adele's body language, Mike barked at her. "Adele that's enough! You can play the blame game later, right now our priority is locating the girls."

Mike did not realize his Lieutenant was standing beside him until he heard him address Adele.

"Hello there Adele. I'm not sure if you remember me.

BLURRED LINE

I'm Lieutenant Jim Nickolas, we met once before at your husband's recognition ceremony. I'm so sorry for what has happened here today, and as I told Mike, I have employed all resources available to me in the hopes of securing a successful outcome."

Pointing in the direction of the street and a large van parked there, they watched as a large antenna began to unfold from the roof of the vehicle.

"I have taken the liberty of calling a friend at Channel Five Cable News, they would like to do a live interview with yourself and Mike. This may help. by increasing the number of eyes looking for the children."

"Okay thank-you Jim, we will do whatever it takes to get our girls back." not looking to see if her husband was following Adele marched towards the news van.

Mike quickly followed in Adele's footsteps, at the same time digging out his wallet and extracting the pictures of Alicia and Desiree.

After Jim, has introduced Mike and Adele to the news crew and while the camera man positioned them, the on-air reporter advised them how she would conduct the interview.

With his camera on his shoulder and pointed at the reporter he silently counts down three fingers then nods to the reporter.

"Good Afternoon this is Rachel Ward at Channel Five Cable News. We are live at the scene where two young girls have been reported missing. I would like to ask Lieutenant Jim Nickolas of the Metro-City Police force to bring us up to speed with what has occurred."

While Jim informed the viewing audience of the event that had occurred, Mike realized that they are amid every parent's worst nightmare, not knowing where their children are. It's like an unexpected blow to the stomach, that leaves you unable to breath.

Feeling a not so subtle kick to his leg, Mike belatedly realized that Rachel had asked him a question.

"I'm sorry what was that?"

BLURRED LINE

"I was wondering if you could show our audience any pictures you may have of the girls?"

Holding up the pictures clutched in his hand, allowing the camera to focus on it, tears ran unchecked from his eyes.

Turning towards Adele, Rachel placed her hand on her arm in a gesture of compassion, turning off her microphone stated. "I have two young boys myself, and if they went missing I would be utterly devastated."

Pointing at the microphone Adele asked her "May I?"

With tears sliding unchecked over her cheeks, Adele poured forth an emotional appeal for the safe return of the girls. The raw emotion apparent in her voice, moved even the operator behind the camera, who has captured all types of human tragedies.

At this point, grasping Mike's hand in her own, and openly sobbing she begs the person responsible to please return the girls to the nearest precinct, and no questions will be asked.

As the reporter winds up the interview and advises her audience to call 9-1-1 in the event they have any information, Mike and Adele still hand in hand, moved away.

Hearing her name being called, Adele see's Maria running towards her, disengaging her hand from Mike's, she steps forward and is immediately embraced by Maria.

Hearing his phone chirp with an incoming call, Mike answered it and heard Larry telling him that Maria told him what has happened and he will be there shortly.

As time seems to race by, and the late afternoon turned into evening, Mike and Adele are increasingly despondent. It is becoming painfully apparent the girls might not be sleeping safe and sound in their own beds tonight. As the Police radio cars, and Police Chopper, call the lieutenant to advise him that they completed a thorough search of a twenty-block radius without success, he reluctantly informed Adele and Mike of this bad news.

BLURRED LINE

Hearing this update from Jim, Adele buried her face in her hands, and with a heart wrenching cry to no one in particular asked. "What do we do now?" with a visible shudder running the length of her body she leaned against Maria for support.

Directing his words towards an equally distraught Mike, Jim advised him that for the time being it might be best if they went home, there is nothing else they can do here.

As the four adults slowly make their way to their vehicles, Adele abruptly stops and turning on her heel, stormed back to Ellen who has remained seated on her front step.

"Just in case you're wondering Ellen, consider yourself fired!" screamed Adele.

CHAPTER SEVEN

The next forty-eight hours were a blur of television and radio interviews for Mike and Adele. As the hours, and days continue to pass-by since their precious daughters were last seen, Mike and Adele appear to be drifting apart in the face of this adversity. It appears that since a quick and successful resolution is not in the offing, the support groups that were initially deeply involved have moved on to new emergencies leaving Mike and Adele to fend for themselves.

On a Sunday morning one week since the girl's disappearance, Mike was sitting at their kitchen table immersed in thought. When Adele joined him at the table, Mike raised his head and noted the uncombed hair, her slumped shoulders, her tired looking eyes confirming that that she has not slept. The pang of guilt Mike felt, as he studied his wife would not recede as he considered the fact that if he had been on time, their lives would not have been altered so drastically. Mike knows that even if their girls were located this very day, the relationship he had enjoyed with Adele, may not survive the trauma of the girl's disappearance. Breaking the uncomfortable silence Mike commented. "I just called Ellen to see if maybe there was some detail she might have forgotten. The operator said the number is no longer in service," adding "The day the girls disappeared the lieutenant was sure he had previously met Ellen but was unable to recall when."

Raising her head, Adele responded. "That's weird, maybe she was getting prank calls."

"Well I was wondering what do we know about Ellen. How did you come to hire her? Did she supply you with references?"

BLURRED LINE

"What are you saying Mike?" Adele asked coldly. "What the fuck Mike? Who's playing the blame game now? You think for a moment I would entrust our daughter's welfare to just anyone? As I remember when I asked you about hiring Ellen, you were so preoccupied with being the super cop you told me to trust my instincts, "with spittle leaking from the corners of her mouth, Adele launched herself from the table and entering their bedroom slammed the door with enough ferocity to make the walls tremble.

Staring at the spot across from him that was so quickly vacated by his wife, Mike quietly murmured. "I was just wondering." That afternoon Mike decided to satisfy his curiosity, driving the short distance to Ellen's, he parked in the driveway and walking up to the door depressed the doorbell hearing it chime inside the residence. Not hearing any movement inside the residence, Mike moved to the living room window that faced the street and cupping his hands to shade his eyes peered inside.

"There's no one home."

Looking around to see who has spoken Mike spotted a frail, rheumy eyed, elderly gentleman leaning on a knobby cane. "I'm sorry. What was that you said?"

"Are you deaf or something? I said there's no one home, are you a peeping Tom, looking in the window like that? I've a good mind to call the police as soon as I get home.!" he warned. Impatiently Mike flipped out his gold Detective shield and advised the geriatric neighbor that he is the police.

"Well why didn't you say so," cackled the old timer.

Walking over to the neighbor Mike asked him. "Where do you live?"

Pointing to the house next door, he explained that he goes for a walk every day at the same time to get away from his cranky wife.

Unable to fully conceal a small grin, Mike then informed him he was looking for Ellen.

"Well she isn't here."

BLURRED LINE

"She's not home today?" queried Mike.

"What's the matter with you? Don't you listen?" exclaimed the old guy. "I said she isn't here, she left three days after, those two girls went missing."

Losing the last of his patience, Mike advised the cranky old timer that unless he stopped talking in riddles, and answered the questions properly Mike would have to arrest him.
Waving his cane in the air at Mike, he demanded to know what he would be arrested for.

Despite is impatience, Mike can't stop the ghost of a smile playing at the corners of his mouth. Shrugging his shoulders Mike answered him. "Perhaps jaywalking."

Observing the highly-animated state of the elderly neighbor, and not wanting to be the cause of a medical emergency, Mike decided to defuse the situation by calmly asking him to relate to Mike what he knew.

With a look of smug satisfaction at Mike's conciliatory tone of voice, the old timer replied. "Three days after the girls went missing, I was out for my usual walk. A car pulled up to the house, some guy got out and went into the house. A short time later him and Ellen came out. I asked her where she was going and if she was alright, the guy told me to mind my own fuckin business. She looked like she was okay and seemed like she knew the guy," then as though anticipating Mike's next question he finished with "She hasn't returned."

Swearing under his breath at this news Mike heard the old guy say.

"Hey, you look familiar. Have you been on T.V?"

"Yes, I'm the missing girl's father."

"I thought so, but you people all look the same to me." Then slowly turning away he tottered off to his home, and cranky wife.

BLURRED LINE

Back in his car Mike vented his anger, slamming the heel of his palm repeatedly against the steering wheel, whilst cursing vociferously.

Returning home to their three-bedroom apartment later that afternoon, Mike notices Adele entering the minuscule spare bedroom. Curious as to what she was doing he approached the doorway and leaning against the door frame asked what she was doing.

"Mike, I will be sleeping in here from now on," she answered in a tone of voice bereft of emotion. As Adele continued to hang clothes in the closet she added. "I feel nothing Mike, do I love you? No. Do I hate you? No. Do I blame you? Yes!"

Turning to face him, and continuing in the same monotone voice. "I will never forgive you for being late. You have cost us everything, our girls, our lives, everything."

Moving from his position against the door frame towards Adele, Mike halted in mid-stride when Adele held up her hand. "No Mike, please, just leave me alone," she murmured with a hint of finality.

Sensing the chasm between himself and Adele won't be bridged by mere words, Mike shrugged his shoulders in resignation and left the room.

The final blow came just two weeks later, when Adele announced that she will be moving out. The three people that Mike loved in the world are now gone. On the rainy Sunday morning that Adele moved the last of her belongings out of the apartment, Mike made one last emotional appeal to her. It was to no avail. As the door closed behind Adele, Mike leaned against the cold metal surface of the door and gave way to the tears filling his eyes, all he ever wanted was a family, and be a successful, respected cop.

Moving restlessly around the apartment, Mike decided that at the first opportunity he will move, as everything that was, is no more.

BLURRED LINE

Opening a cupboard, he spied several bottles of Whiskey, picking one up he twirled the bottle admiring the amber color as the light touches it. "What the Hell, it's been a long time." he stated out loud to break the deafening silence. Plucking a glass from the counter, Mike moved the couch in the Livingroom and poured a large drink into the tumbler.

CHAPTER EIGHT

Hearing an annoying buzz, and trying to decipher where it's originating from, Mike slowly regained consciousness. He becomes aware of something tickling his nose, painfully opening his eyes, he realizes that he is face down on the living room carpet, muttering "What the fuck?". Then as his pounding brain begins to sift through the alcohol induced fog, he realizes that he needs to get to the bathroom. Mike's not sure how he managed to get to the toilet in time, all he knows is that he carried on a one-sided conversation with the toilet for the next thirty minutes. The inside of his mouth tastes like stale whiskey mixed with residual vomit. Rising from his uncomfortable position cradling the toilet, and barely able to stay upright he managed to turn on the cold water tap. His stomach muscles were cramping in protest from the unrelenting retching. Closing his eyes, he cups water with his hands and splashes it on his face, shivering as the shock of cold water registered with his be-fogged brain. Reaching for the glass located on the side of the sink, Mike fills it with cold water and taking a swig of it begins to rid the vile taste from his mouth.

Looking at himself in the mirror, he absorbed the bloodshot eyes, the stubble on his face again muttering "What the fuck?" Slowly and painfully navigating his way back to the living room Mike was dumbfounded to see empty Pizza boxes, as well as empty Chinese food take out cartons, strewn about the room. Then seeing something that might be the T.V remote peeking out from under an empty pizza box, Mike retrieves it and turns off the annoying buzz.

BLURRED LINE

Picking up an empty whiskey bottle that was perched precariously on the coffee table, shaking his head in disbelief, took the empty bottle into the kitchen. Mike then noticed another empty whiskey bottle in the kitchen sink, nestled comfortably beside an empty vodka bottle. "Jesus Christ" he muttered. Pressing his palms against his temples in a futile attempt to ease the pounding, Mike wondered what day it was. Turning on the small television in the kitchen, Mike tunes into a local news station and is alarmed to see that it is now six am Wednesday. "Shit I lost three days," he muttered out loud. Deciding that his stomach and head are not able to withstand the rigors of cleaning up the apartment, he headed for a hot shower.

Feeling minutely better for the shower, and dressed in shirt and tie, Mike retrieved his gun from the safe, donning a pair of sunglasses, and clipping his Detective shield to his belt headed out the door.

Mike's boss Lieutenant Jim Nickolas, has so far been more than accommodating during these last 3 months, allowing Mike the time needed to attend to his personal issues. Pushing through the revolving Precinct door Mike can only hope that he still has a job. Mike doesn't bother to stop and check in with desk Sergeant O'Mallory, a man that he feels only contempt for. As Mike wends his way through the congested main floor of the precinct he heard O'Mallory's cigarette roughened voice call out to him.

"Hey Chance you look like shit!"

"Ya screw you O'Mallory, at least my ass hasn't been glued to the same chair for twenty years, "snapped Mike, pushing through the doorway entering the relative sanctuary of the stairwell.

Arriving at the second-floor Detectives room Mike was immediately waved into his boss Lieutenant Jim Nickolas office.

"Nice of you to join us again Mike," growled Jim.

"I'm really sorry about this Lieutenant," apologized Mike. Pushing back from his desk Jim looked up at Mike and shaking his head declared.

"You look like shit Mike."

BLURRED LINE

Looking somewhat abashed, Mike answered. "Ya so I've been told," explaining. "Adele moved out on Sunday morning, guess I figured the solution to my problem was at the bottom of a bottle."

Gazing at Mike with empathy Jim remarked. "Mike I feel for you. I was hoping that you and Adele would be able to get through this. I remember when my first wife left, I too thought my world had ended." Closing his eyes and leaning back in his chair, Jim appeared to be lost in thought at the same time tapping his pen on the desk, then re-opening his eyes says to Mike. "I want you to know Mike that I fully commiserate with your situation, and what has befallen you. Unfortunately, I cannot properly manage this department if personnel fail to show up for shifts, or as in your case fail to advise me that you're not available for work. Therefore, with this in mind I would like to suggest that I arrange some meetings with yourself and Jackie Nelson."

"Jackie Nelson? the department's shrink," enquired Mike.

"Well some call her that, I prefer to call her a counselor. Let's face it Mike, in the last three months you have had a significant amount of trauma in your life. Now these visits are not to be considered mandated by the Department. Myself I feel strongly that you may benefit from seeing her," concluded Jim in a fatherly tone of voice.

CHAPTER NINE

Moving through the revolving doors of the twelfth precinct at 7:45 am Monday morning, Mike smiled at the ever-present chaos. The barrage of noise is continuous as perpetrators in handcuffs noisily proclaim their innocence to anyone who might listen.

Leaving the chaos behind as he ascends the staircase to the second-floor detective's division, Mike felt his cell phone vibrate with an incoming call. Plucking the phone from his pants pocket and glancing at the number, sees it's his partner Larry on the detective squad. Remaining in the quiet of the staircase to take the call Mike answered the call.

"Hey Mike I have to take a couple of days off to clear up some things."

"Okay no problem," replied Mike "But what about the lieutenant, what should I tell him?"

"Tell that pompous asshole to open the window of his office jump out, and see how long it takes him to hit the ground."

Smiling at the thought of this scenario Mike responded "Well I guess I won't say that but I will let him know you're not in for a couple of days."

"Thanks Mike."

Arriving at his desk Mike prepared himself to sit his large framed body into what must be the world's most uncomfortable chair, he is sure this chair was an instrument of torture in a past life. Plucking the first file off a small mountain of files that require his attention he is soon completely immersed into the lives of two brothers named Charlie, and Vinnie Delveccio.

BLURRED LINE

Every time he reads this file, Mike is astounded by the fact that there is nothing these two won't do, suspected in everything from petty Larceny to Murder. Mike is starting to question the fact that they have never even seen the inside of a courtroom, they have been arrested many times on suspicion but always released due to lack of evidence, or witnesses re-canting their stories. The retiring Detective who turned this file over to him extracted a solemn promise from Mike, that he will do everything in his power to ensure these brothers are put behind bars where they belong. At least once a month Mike visits the drinking establishments that the brothers are known to frequent. With his gold, detective shield in plain view for all to see, he advises the patrons he is after the Delveccio brothers. He also tells them that the brothers need not look over their shoulders as they won't see him coming until it's too late.

Sensing a presence beside him, Mike reluctantly tears his eyes away from the file and looks up to see his Lieutenant looming over his desk.

"Morning Mike, how are you?" asked Jim.

"Morning yourself Lieutenant, not bad for a Monday." Jerking his thumb in the direction of the empty chair at Larry's desk Mike relayed the fact that Larry will not be in.

"Well nice of him to let me know," muttered Jim. Then in the same breath asked Mike "What are you working on?"

"Just wondering how these fucking Delveccios seem to avoid any charges, there is something about this whole file that is starting to stink," replied Mike thoughtfully.

Then remembering the reason why he's at Mike's desk Jim asked 'Hey where are you at with that report I asked for?"

Waving at the stack of files on his desk and with a small grin, Mike informed Jim "I'm sure it's here somewhere."

"Well I would like to have it before the end of the day." hen as though searching for something else to say continued to stand in front of Mike's desk.

BLURRED LINE

"I better take this boss," Mike states pointing at the blinking light on his desk phone and with relief Mike watched as Jim turned away towards his office.

Watching Jim head towards his office, it was clear to Mike that Jim had something else he had wanted to speak about, shrugging it off for now, Mike answered his desk phone.

"Good Morning Mike, this is Jackie Nelson."

Swearing under his breath upon hearing this name, Mike maintained a cool, courteous voice, when he asked how he can help her.

"Well Mike you missed the three o'clock appointment we had set for last Friday."

Mike patiently informed Jackie, that even though he has been seeing her on a regular basis for three months now, it does not alter the fact that he has lost his children, and his wife, because he fucked up. "I didn't miss that appointment; I believe you made that appointment even though I told you that I would not be there, nor would I be attending any further appointments with you."

After about four long heartbeats Mike heard Jackie's reply "Well I'm sorry to hear that Mike, I had thought we were making very real progress."

Upon hearing this Mike interrupted her. "That's it exactly Jackie, you thought we were making progress, myself, I'm not so sure. I appreciate your taking the time to help me work through this, but in the final analysis, I must accept responsibility.

Retaining her calm, professional demeanor Jackie replied. "If that's the way you feel then I will forward my report to your Lieutenant."

Glancing around the office to see if this call has attracted any unwanted attention, and satisfied that no one was listening, Mike cautiously asked "Wait a minute Jackie why are you forwarding a report to Jim? My visits to you were not mandated by the department, it was only suggested that I see you."

BLURRED LINE

"This is true Mike, and what we discussed will of course remain confidential, but the department asked me to determine your operational status. In other words, are you a danger to yourself, or others while on duty."

Attempting to keep his tone from revealing his anger, that perhaps his boss miss-lead him Mike asked "So what did you find Jackie? Am I fit for duty?"

"Oh, I can't answer that Mike, that information will be in the report I forward to Jim."

In a voice dripping with sarcasm Mike replied "Well you do what you have to do Jackie and thanks for nothing." Exerting unparalleled self-control, Mike carefully replaced the handset into its cradle, instead of launching it across the room.

Cradling his head in his hands while counting to ten, Mike waited for his heart rate to drop back to normal. Sensing a return to normal body rhythms Mike began to rummage through the files searching for the unfinished report his boss had asked for. Muttering "Hell with it" Mike was surprised to find himself out of his chair, and on his way to the lieutenant's office.

Not bothering to knock or otherwise announce his presence, Mike committed the cardinal sin of simply walking in, closing the door, and leaning back against it.

Taking his time before looking up to see who has committed the serious offense of entering his office without permission, Jim finally looked up and seeing Mike stated "You better have a good reason for this intrusion Chance!"

Lacking any trace of warmth in his voice, Mike asked Jim. "Why the fuck do you want a report from Jackie?"

Not bothering to pretend ignorance about either Jackie or the report, Jim leaned back in his chair and waving at the only other chair in the office invited Mike to sit down. Ignoring the gesture Mike shrugged his shoulders and remarked "I'll stand."

BLURRED LINE

Pointing out to the room full of detectives Jim remarked. "I know all you guys think I'm in this position because of my family connections.

That might very well be but in the meantime," and in voice carved from granite continued. "It is my responsibility to ensure that the people I send out to Protect and Serve the good citizens of Metro-City, aren't more of threat to them than the actual criminals are. I don't give a rat's ass if someone's feelings are hurt in the process, continuing to glare at Mike he remarked. "Just between you me I have served my retirement papers, and thankfully I will be out of here in a month. I will no longer have to pander to a bunch of egocentric detectives and their bullshit personalities, we're done here Mike, now get the fuck out my office." As Mike wends his way back to his desk he wonders if Jim will be asking for his gun and badge, based on whatever Jackie feels she needs to put in her report. Sitting back down at his desk he notices some of the detectives who were still sitting at their desks, and witnessed his transgression, were grinning at him and a few others gave him the thumbs up.

Feeling somewhat mollified he located the report that Jim was hounding him for, giving it his full attention, he is soon lost in a maze of numbers regarding the many different crimes that people commit against each other.

Hearing the quiet buzz of his cell phone vibrating, Mike smiled as he watched it vibrate its way across his desk. Not really wanting to talk to anyone Mike decided to let his voice mail take the call.

Realizing the time, Mike was not surprised to feel his stomach rumble, deciding that his stomach is not to be ignored Mike retrieves his gun from the desk drawer, and slides it into his belt holster. Grabbing his jacket, he heads for the stairwell already anticipating the hot and spicy dishes at Miguel's Mexican restaurant just two short blocks away.

BLURRED LINE

Pushing through the door to the first floor, and the constant bedlam there-in, Mike remembers his two years as a patrolman, and how he had loved the atmosphere and action. Shaking his head, Mike now wonders how anyone could stand all this noise, hearing his name bellowed out over the other fifty voices, Mike was annoyed to see O'Mallory waving him over to his desk.

"Shit," Mike muttered as he reluctantly changed direction and headed over to O'Mallory's desk.

Approaching O'Mallory's raised desk, Mike finds the Sergeant with the phone wedged between his shoulder and ear, while at the same time hastily scribbling on a legal pad. Simultaneously hanging up the phone, and tearing the page from the pad, O'Mallory took a moment to study what he had written down, then almost reluctantly handed it to Mike with a gruff "This might be of interest to you."

CHAPTER TEN

Moving to a quiet corner of the room before attempting to read the Sergeant's childlike scribble, Mike happened to look back over his shoulder and noticed O'Mallory staring at him. Mike looked back down at the note and began to decipher the sergeant's note.

Pedestrian involved Hit and Run, one fatality, documents found in victim's purse tentatively identify the victim as one Maria Donovan, accident scene is located at First Avenue and 24th street. All thoughts of hot and spicy Mexican food at Miguel's, disappeared like morning mist in a hot sun as Mike re-read the short paragraph. Then with complete disregard for others, he violently pushed his way through the crowded foyer to the exit. While Mike was fighting his way through the busy foyer, he's completely oblivious to the fact that the malevolent filled eyes of Sergeant O'Mallory are tracking his progress. Mike might have also found it curious if he had witnessed O'Mallory quickly place a personal call on his cell phone, then speaking only a couple of words ended the call.

Arriving at the underground parking spot where he parks his on-duty car, Mike was highly annoyed to find it empty. Muttering a single explosive expletive, at the same time checking to see if he had maybe parked it in the wrong spot, Mike happened to see the parking attendant. With the deceptively fast, ground eating strides that his six foot three inch, two hundred and thirty-five-pound frame is capable of. Mike approached the attendant and with elevated feelings of annoyance, and frustration at the unnecessary delay Mike hollered. "Where in the fuck is my car?"

BLURRED LINE

Then feeling instantly contrite when the attendant turned to face him, and Mike discovered that she is a young lady who looks to be only about twenty-five years old. "I apologize for that outburst, but I have an emergency to get to," Mike explained.

Seeming to understand, she surprised Mike with what sounded like an Australian accent when she responded. "No worries, and you are?"

After Mike identified himself, she looked at her clipboard and reaching into her pants pocket extracted a set of keys, handing them to Mike stated "Your car is getting some service work completed, so here take the car from slot forty-five as it won't be needed until tomorrow," tossing a casual, "Good day" over her shoulder began walking away.

Mike offered a perfunctory thank-you then turned away and hurried to get the car, fuming at the delay Mike slapped the red emergency beacon onto the car roof and turning it on, accelerated out of the garage and headed to the scene of the hit and run. Upon arriving at the scene Mike was not at all surprised to see a crowd of onlookers, they seem to be drawn to scenes of death and destruction like moths to a flame. Not caring that he has double parked, Mike flips down the sun visor identifying the vehicle as police, then checks to make sure his gold detective shield is visible, spotting a patrolman looking impatiently around for help, headed over to him.

"Hey Detective you took your time getting here me and my partner haven't even had lunch yet, it's all yours now." and with that he turns on his heel as if to walk away.

"Hold it right there," barked Mike. "It's not my case I'm just here to confirm the identity of the victim."

As the patrolman turned back to face him, Mike glanced at the name badge, "Hey Lance you're worried about your fuckin lunch?" queried Mike. Then unable to control himself, he continued in a voice that clearly indicated his contempt for Lance's complete disregard for the victim.

BLURRED LINE

"You do realize that a human being is lying under that cover over there, they will never again enjoy a lunch or a hug or see loved ones. All their hopes and dreams have just ended abruptly. Your compassion for the victim is touching," concluded Mike in a voice leaden with derision.

Not displaying any outward appearance of discomfiture at Mike's obvious scorn, Patrolman Lance shrugged his shoulders and casually replied "Not me under the tarp detective."

Realizing that he was wasting good air attempting to appeal to Lance's sense of compassion, Mike asked him where his partner was.

Lance indicated the guy holding up the side of the patrol car with his back.

"Okay well, tell you what if this was my file I would have you guys get the perimeter tape, and I would want it to include the whole area. This means that you must direct traffic for the next 3 hours or so, then your partner can work the crowd to see if anyone saw what happened. Pointing a finger at some morbid son of bitch with a camera over the tarp enshrouded victim, Mike informed Lance that he could begin by getting him the fuck out of the crime scene."

"But what about lunch?" whined Lance.

With a sardonic grin, Mike, replied innocently "Well there's always tomorrow, right," and with that he headed over to perform the task he's been dreading. Approaching the tarp shrouded victim Mike slowly crouched down, and with great reluctance peeled back just enough of the tarp to reveal the victim's face, the impact of what he sees rocks him to his core. Inhaling short breaths desperately not wanting to believe what his eyes are telling him, he gazes upon the battered and bloody face of his partner's wife. Maria's unseeing eyes are gazing at something only the deceased can see.

BLURRED LINE

With granular pebbles from the pavement, ingrained into her face like random flakes of black pepper, the devastation to her face caused by the sudden, hard impact with the unyielding pavement was catastrophic. Any resemblance to the beautiful, vivacious, lady who had just had him over three nights ago, for supper, was no longer visible, with an overpowering sense of melancholy, Mike slowly lowered the tarp to once again cover Maria.

Regaining his feet Mike forced his mind to slow down, and think about what needs to be done and the order they need to be done in. With his eyes still transfixed on the tarp, he reached for his cell phone to call Larry, when the generic computer generated voice advised Mike that the call cannot be completed he decided to try Larry at home. Mike was unprepared to hear Maria's soft, lilting voice on the pre-taped voice message, badly shaken, his mind attempted to reconcile the fact that the owner of the voice message is lying broken and deceased in the street. Deciding that he should reach out to his boss and let him know what's happening, Mike made the call "Hey Boss its Mike Chance calling, I'm down here at First Ave and Twenty-fourth street."

"What the hell are you doing down their Mike, and where is that report I have been asking you for?" demanded Jim.

Explaining to his boss what has occurred, and who the victim is seemed to somewhat mollify his boss, then Mike advised him what he had the reluctant patrolman doing.

Mike enquired "Who will catch this file boss so I can get them up to speed?"

Following a short pause Jim answered "Since you're already their Mike, and you have initiated the investigation, consider it yours."

"But boss, the victim is a good friend and the wife of my partner," protested Mike vehemently.

"Consider that to be a motivator to quickly solve this.'

Prepared to argue further Mike was cut short when he heard the call dis-connected.

BLURRED LINE

Now finding himself having to switch mental gears from being a friend of the victim, to the lead investigator. Mike glanced down at the deceased Maria, making a solemn promise to bring the perpetrator to justice. Seeing the black Medical examiners wagon pull up to the scene, Mike absently wonders who has been dispatched to cover this. It is with a sense of relief that he recognizes the gum chewing Melody Webster, who is ferocious when investigating a case. Leaving no stone unturned, a through professional whose motto is "Only the facts please." Watching Mel and her assistant don the white paper suits to protect their clothes, as well as the integrity of the crime scene,
Mike walked over and advise her of the identity of the victim. "Afternoon Mel," Mike called as he approached her.

Looking up at Mike, and taking three heartbeats to study his face, she responded "It's Mike, right? didn't we work that case together about a year ago?"

Nodding his head in assent Mike began without preamble "The victim's name is Maria Donovan."

"Hold on a sec Mike." reaching into her car Mel brought forth a clipboard with attached papers and began filling in the victim's name.

Slowly looking back up at Mike, she repeats the name "Maria Donovan, Uh Mike that's your partners last name if memory serves me right, any relation to him?"

"His wife," murmured a somber Mike.

"Jesus Christ, Mike that really sucks," pausing as she slowly digested this information, asked Mike if he knew what dumb ass detective she must work this case with.

Watching to see if the patrolmen were following his orders, Mike looked back at Mel answering her question. "Ya that would be me Mel."

BLURRED LINE

Looking at Mike, all five foot three inches of Melody seemed to explode with anger declaring. "Seriously Mike, that asshole of a boss of yours is going to have you investigate the death of your partner's wife?" shaking her head in disgust Mel asked him if he can refuse.

Staring into the distance at nothing, Mike slowly shook his head, then as if talking to himself answered Mel "At first I felt the same way Mel, but I have made a promise to Maria that I will find whoever did this to her and see them brought to justice."

Absorbing what Mike said Mel nods in the affirmative and softly murmurs "I hear ya."

Then, surprising Mike with what she did next, she placed her warm, tiny hand on his bare forearm, informing Mike that she's aware of what Mike has been through, and hoped that he was doing alright considering the circumstances.

Seeing the tiny hand on his arm, Mike was almost too astonished by what Mel has done to answer, then finding his tongue he replied with a heartfelt "Thank-you for that Mel, I'm dealing with it."

CHAPTER ELEVEN

Moving away so that Mel and her assistant can initiate their investigation, Mike returned to the immediate area of impact, and was dismayed to see both of Maria's shoes lying in the middle of the marked cross walk. This was the point where they became removed from the feet they were meant to adorn. Deciding that he needed a different vantage point to perhaps gain a better insight to the accident, grinning like a wolf at Patrolman Lance swearing as he directed traffic, Mike hurried across the intersection. Gaining the far sidewalk, he looked back towards the scene, and immediately felt something niggling his subconscious, something obvious yet at the same time hidden. Unable to decipher what his subconscious was attempting to tell him, Mike resorted to an old trick he was taught by a retiring detective. Turning his head away from the scene, he allowed his eyes to come to rest upon a very pregnant lady, who with clearly discernible love, gently massaging her swollen abdomen.

Gazing back at the scene Mike was frustrated to find that he remains stymied, unable to grasp what should be obvious. Slowly turning his head slightly to widen the scope of his vision, realization slowly dawned on him as to what he was missing. The Panhandler, the unseen observers, this small, but growing segment of society whose existence is largely ignored by all others.

Mike now remembers seeing this same guy, wearing the distinctive camouflage jacket, at several different intersections around Metro-city.

BLURRED LINE

Deciding to play a hunch Mike headed in the direction of the panhandler, at the same time pulling a ten-dollar bill as well as a twenty-dollar bill from his wallet and placing them in his shirt pocket.

Arriving at the outstretched legs of the panhandler, who looked very comfortable with his back against the wall of a bank, basking in the warmth of the early May sun.

Feeling a presence stopped in front of him, the Panhandler raised his face to Mike, displaying two eyes with pupils the color of milk.

Nodding at him, Mike politely enquired if he was having a good day.

"Ya not bad," was the noncommittal reply.

Considering the hat set out for donations, Mike decided to set a trap. "Those two bills in your hat look lonely." He was instantly rewarded when he heard the snap of the trap jaws come together.

"Ya just a couple of George Washington's," then realizing what he had said, quickly tried to cover up his blunder with the fact that the kind people who had donated the money, told him all they had could spare were dollar bills.

Grinning widely Mike informed the panhandler "I don't give a shit if you want to make your living by having others feel sorry for you. Pretending to be blind with those contact lenses, that's on you, but maybe you can help me." Pointing to his shield in case the panhandler had somehow missed it, Mike squatted down to be eye level with the Panhandler, pointing a thumb over his shoulder towards the intersection where Maria was killed.

BLURRED LINE

"I am investigating a hit and run fatality, and I wonder given your location if you witnessed anything?" at the same time extracting the ten-dollar bill from his pockct.

Gazing at the proffered money, he mentioned to Mike that although he really likes Alexander Hamilton, he has a greater fondness for Andrew Jackson

Sensing that he may have hit pay dirt, Mike asked him what his name is.

"Henry," is the one-word answer.

"Well Henry if you can help me out here, Alexander happens to have a friend with him named Andrew."

"Got your pen and paper detective?"

Not sure what Henry might have to offer Mike decided to humor him, extracting his crumbled notepad from his pants pocket, and a pen from his shirt pocket he advised Henry to proceed. It was like a thumb was pulled out of a dyke, and the water started to flow as Henry began to speak.

"Well, the street was busy with cars coming and going with everyone in a hurry trying to beat the lights all the time. There weren't a lot of pedestrians as you can tell." nodding disgustingly at his hat, then taking a breath continued. "At the time, I never gave it a thought as cars park all the time at the meters with no one getting out. For some reason a black Nissan Sentra parked, but the driver kept hitting the gas pedal I dunno, maybe it wanted to stall. Anyway, there were no pedestrians until this beautiful lady showed up, she waited for the light to change, then started to cross the intersection coming towards me." seeming to ponder his next words for a heartbeat he pointed towards where the Nissan had parked and continued "Then I heard a godawful roar as the driver in the Nissan floored the engine and hit that lady, I never thought a body could fly that far."

Hearing this vivid description of Maria's final moments alive, has shaken Mike and he was barely able to maintain his composure when he prompted Henry "Anything else?"

BLURRED LINE

"Ya the driver stopped and got out of the vehicle and looked at her."

"What did he look like?" prompted Mike.

"Short blonde hair, about six foot three, six foot four about three hundred pounds," replied Henry.

"Jesus Henry, you're pretty observant for a blind guy."

"Really Detective what else am I going to do sitting here all day, not like I have any money to count." waving at the offending hat.

Regaining his feet, wincing as his knees cracked, Mike asked a final question." Get a plate number Henry?"

"Didn't have one," was the terse reply. "Hey Detective don't forget Andrew."

Reaching into his pocket and placing Alexander and Andrew together, Mike leaned down as though to place them in the hat.

"Whoa their Detective, I'll take those, put them in the hat and some fucking thief will steal them when I'm not looking."

At least now Mike has a description of the suspect vehicle and heads back to where Mel and her assistant were wrapping up their investigation

"Everything done here Mel?" Mike enquired as they removed their white suits.

"Yes Mike, I will send you a copy of the autopsy report as soon as its complete."

"Thanks Mel." Making his way over to Patrolman Lance, Mike advised him that the perimeter tape can come down and him and his partner are free to go. Taking one last look at the immediate area to ensure nothing was missed, Mike headed over to his car and looking at his watch is surprised to see it's already five pm, pulling out his cell phone he attempted to reach Larry. Strangely enough Mike felt a sense of relief there is no answer, although he knows that at some point in time he will have tell his friend the worst possible news he will ever hear. Tilting his head back against the headrest in the car, Mike closed his eyes, ruminating about what Henry had witnessed. Opening his eyes and starting the car he mused out loud "Can't hurt to look."

CHAPTER TWELVE

It took only fifteen minutes driving time, but it appears Mike has crossed some sort of line, as the area he has now entered bears a striking resemblance to what Armageddon must look like. Driving through two open chain link gates that must be ten feet high, with a clearly marked sign declaring these premises to be the property of. "Alfred's Auto Crushing and Re-Cycling, all visitors must remain in their vehicles and report to the office." Mike entered an incredibly decrepit industrial yard littered with skeletons of cars scattered randomly about, and drove slowly towards the office, Mike has had official police business before at this address, and is familiar with both the business and its disreputable owner. This business is well known to law enforcement, as vehicles that need to disappear with no questions asked, end up here. Fully aware that there are eyes watching him, and they have likely already made him as a cop, Mike knew that he had entered an environment where his longevity is not guaranteed. Opening his door, Mike cautiously stepped out of his vehicle, his hearing is instantly assaulted with a cacophony of screeching metal, as though it were being tortured, combined with the roar of a diesel motor.

Cringing at the continuing eardrum splitting screech, Mike was unaware that he was not alone, and almost jumped when he heard over the riot of sound, someone growling at his shoulder. "What the fuck do you want?"

BLURRED LINE

Turning to face the voice, Mike immediately noticed that the person speaking to him has in his right hand, a steel wrench of some kind that could clearly cause serious damage if used as a weapon. Ensuring the wrench bearing voice was watching, Mike moved his right hand and placed it on his hip, in close proximity to his weapon. Feeling more secure knowing that he is now able to quickly grasp his weapon, Mike took a long five seconds to study the owner of the voice. With a bulbous head seemingly attached directly to the shoulders, and a body roughly five feet tall and just about as wide. This wrench bearing person is wearing what must be the filthiest pair of cover-all's Mike has ever seen, he was barely able to discern the name tag identifying the wearer as Gary.

"What you planning on doing with that Gary?" yelled Mike pointing at the wrench.

Staring at Mike with undisguised hatred, Gary calmly began to tap the large wrench against his empty hand. "Depends on you," he grunted quietly as the sudden cessation of tortured metal allowed for normal conversation levels.

Hearing the office door open, and wanting to put some distance between himself and the wrench wielding Gary. Mike turned and starts walking towards the approaching person, whom he recognized as the owner of these questionable premises. Stopping about six feet from Mike, and waving at Gary telling him "I got this, you can go," he continued to watch until Gary had ponderously disappeared into another building.

Returning his vulture like gaze to Mike, absorbing the details of the gold shield and weapon, Alfred cordially enquired "Are you lost detective?"

Not bothering to introduce himself, Mike informed Alfred that he was searching for a black, four door Nissan Sentra.

BLURRED LINE

Chuckling Alfred answered "Being a detective you should know that you need to go to a car dealership to find such a vehicle."

"Let me be more specific Alfred, I'm looking for a vehicle that was involved in a fatal hit and run, and was reported by an eye witness to be a black four door Nissan Sentra. I have reason to believe this vehicle may have ended up here for disposal."

"Well that raises an interesting problem detective, you don't happen to have a warrant by any chance, do you?" drawled Alfred with a smirk that Mike would have loved to remove. Winking at Mike, Alfred continued. "You know there just might have been one of those today, I'm not really an authority on makes and models of vehicles." Then shrugging his shoulders declared vehemently. "Without a search warrant Mike, you're screwed!"

Disguising the surprise, he felt at the use of his first name, Mike responded with a smirk of his own. "Appears you remember me Alfred."

No longer pretending to be cordial Alfred snarled "Yea you're the asshole that had me shut down for a month, and cost me a ton of money, now get in your car and get the fuck off my property!"

Still grinning as he walked nonchalantly towards his vehicle, Mike can't help himself when he advised Alfred that lightning does, and will strike twice in the same place.

Watching Mike drive away, Alfred spun on his heel, and with short choppy steps headed back to his office, and where upon entering sees a blonde giant of a figure peering out through the lone dirty window.

"What the fuck are you doing Vinnie?" What if he had seen you?"

"Shit this window is so dirty it's like looking through mud, there was no way he was going to see me," declared Vinnie turning to face Alfred.

BLURRED LINE

Sitting down at his desk, Alfred leaned back in his chair and closing his eyes muttered. "That was close Vinnie, way too fucking close, tell your boss I'm done."

"Hey asshole you get paid good money for doing this stuff, so don't start fuckin whining now." Then with a final warning look at him Vinnie left the office, slipping around to the back of the office and was picked up by older brother Charlie, in a decrepit Ford pick-up truck.

Arriving back at the gates to the property, Mike was not in the least bit surprised to see the squat form of Gary waiting there to close them. The wrench appears to have become a part of Gary's right hand, as he still retains possession of the large wrench. Denying himself the satisfaction of shoving that wrench of Gary's where the sun doesn't shine, Mike instead flips his middle finger up at him as he drives through the gates.

Driving back into the city, Mike can't help but utter a single explosive expletive simultaneously slamming the steering wheel with his open hand, frustrated knowing that with the disappearance of the Black Nissan, now nothing short of a confession by the guilty party will allow him to fulfill his promise to Maria.

Hearing a growl emit from the immediate area of his stomach, Mike glanced at his watch and was amazed to see it's already six pm. Twenty minutes later he parked his vehicle at a popular fast foot diner, and was heading inside when he felt his phone vibrate with an incoming call.

Mike's low key "Hello Larry" was drowned out by Larry's rich contagious laugh, asking Mike if perhaps he missed Larry as his number has shown up a few times.

"Where in the hell are you Larry, Timbuktu?"

"Ya just about Mike, I'm over here in South-bend."

"What are you doing there?" asks a puzzled Mike.

"Well you know I am from here, funny thing though I couldn't get out of this hick town fast enough once I had graduated.

BLURRED LINE

About a month ago, I received a letter from the mayor asking me if I would be interested in the Police Chiefs job as the current Police Chief had passed away.

Maria and I had talked about it, thinking that we might like to move away from the crime in the city.

We decided that I should come look. By the way Mike, have you been talking to Maria today? I've been trying to call her all day to ask her to come here as well as, but it just goes to her voice mail."

Leaning his back against the tree outside of the diner as if attempting to gain support for what he was about to do, Mike took a deep breath, then informed Larry about all that has transpired on this fateful day.

When he has finished telling Larry, the only sound Mike heard was his own heart beating. After about thirty seconds of the type of silence reserved for cemetery's, Larry quietly told Mike "I'm on my way home."

CHAPTER THIRTEEN

Sitting at his desk on a dreary Wednesday morning, Detective Mike Chance could hardly believe the changes that have occurred in the month since Maria Donovan's death. Recalling the painful phone call to his estranged wife Adele, whom he had not talked to in over four months, advising her of Maria's passing and the funeral details. Mike was filled with trepidation at the thought of encountering Adele at the funeral, and was relieved when the hug she gave him was as perfunctory as one given to a new acquaintance. Soon after the funeral, Larry announced to Mike that he was going to accept that opportunity in South-Bend, he finds it too painful remaining where he is being reminded daily, of the loss of his wife and best friend. Hearing a commotion Mike looked over to see Lieutenant Bill Watson, who replaced the now retired Lieutenant Jim Nickolas, enter the room with his ever-present entourage in tow.

Sensing the futility of the exercise, but unable to stop himself Mike re-opened the file from the Medical Examiner's Office. Scouring the details provided in the report by the gum chewing Melody Webster, he realized that Maria's death won't be solved by reading a report. Checking to see that his gun was secured in its holster, he decides to go apply some pressure to a pair of brothers.

Pulling into the parking area at Jo's Bar and Grill, Mike was not surprised to see half a dozen cars already parked there. This seedy, rundown, eyesore of a bar is well known to the police as a favorite hangout for those who have questionable sources of income. The high volume of illicit drug sales continues within this bar, despite the best efforts of the police to curtail it.

BLURRED LINE

Exiting his car Mike noticed the two small dumpsters located by a rundown fence, were overflowing to the point that the debris piled around the bins acts as a ladder for the rats to access their buffet.

Entering the dark enclave of the bar, Mike's nostrils are immediately assailed by the acrid smell of burning cigarettes, and over flowing ashtrays. In contrast to the bright sun outside, the meager light afforded by the few working lights of the common room, compelled Mike to remain in the shadows until his eyes adjusted. As the interior of the bar slowly took shape he sees tables randomly scattered about a moderately sized room, and seated in the farthest corner of the room spots his quarry. Having apparently garnered no interest from the current assortment of patrons seated at the tables, Mike continued to stand in the shadows, and survey the room. Feeling somewhat vulnerable as he does not yet have a new partner to replace Larry, he decides on a course of action that may slightly tip the odds back in his favor.

Moving from the relative sanctuary of the shadows, into the only marginally better light, Mike instantly felt the eyes of the bartender tracking him like a cat with an unsuspecting mouse. Taking in the gold shield clipped to Mike's belt, and the gun on his right hip, the bartender nervously looks around as though seeking help from some unidentifiable source. Approaching the bar Mike observed the thin, greasy blonde hair, and deeply pockmarked face of the bartender, whose lips are home to a burning cigarette.

Arriving at the bar counter, and much to the chagrin of the bartender, Mike took his time studying the much-abused bar top, observing the countless burn marks from cigarettes. Finally looking at the bartender, Mike was secretly pleased to note beads of sweat breaking out on the forehead of the bartender.

"What's your name?" enquired Mike nonchalantly.

BLURRED LINE

"Blake," growled the bartender, his right eye squinting at Mike as the rising tendril of smoke issuing from the cigarette irritated it. Accompanying Blake's voice, is a foul smell that can only be associated with the few remaining, and visibly rotting stumps of teeth he possesses.

"Well Blake," "I can see by my watch that it's time for your fifteen-minute break and I would suggest that you take it outside."

Unfolding his crossed arms from his chest, thereby exposing what appear to be bad jailhouse tattoos on each arm, Blake leaned towards Mike, and in a voice attempting to masquerade his nervousness with false bravado demanded "Who the fuck are you to tell me when my breaks are asshole?"

Chuckling at this outburst, Mike pointed to the gold Detective shield on his belt responding icily. "I'm the guy that can make your life completely miserable. One short phone call I can have this place swarming with people that will ask you really awkward questions about those little bags of white powder under your bar."

"Time for my break, I will be back in fifteen minutes," announced Blake to an apparently uncaring clientele, and with a final glare at Mike headed into the back room.

Waiting for a minute to ensure Blake did not attempt to sneak back, Mike heads over to confront the Delveccio brothers. Arriving at their table staring first at the older brother Charlie, then fixing his stare on Vinnie. Noticing that each brother had a full glass of beer on the table in front of them, Mike casually reached out and tipped each one over so the cold contents run off the table and onto their laps. Jumping up from their chairs with a collective yelp of surprise, mixed with anger they hollered "What the fuck?"

Stepping back a pace from these now enraged giants, Mike calmly states, "Looks like you pissed yourselves boys."

"Fuck you cop, you spilled our beer on us!" shouted Vinnie.

BLURRED LINE

Jerking his thumb towards the door and the street outside Mike chuckled, replying "They don't know that, now sit the fuck back down," all traces of humor disappearing from Mike's voice. Taking time to quickly glance around the room to see if the commotion caused any undue interest, Mike smiled when he spotted four of the patrons beating a hasty retreat to the exit sign. Turning his attention back to the brothers, and older brother Charlie's reptilian stare, Mike began to speak in a voice that was leaden with poison. "Know this boys, I am coming after you, don't bother to look over your shoulder for me because you won't see me coming. I don't make threats, I make promises, and I promise that you will be either dead, or in prison for the rest of your lives." Aware of the description of the driver in the Nissan resembles Vinnie, he decided to fire a shot in the dark to see what, if anything resulted from it. "There was a hit and run fatality about a month ago, and the suspect vehicle was reported by an eye witness to be a four-door black Nissan Sentra."

Looking up at Mike, Vinnie stupidly began to protest "There was no one," and was savagely interrupted by Charlie ordering Vinnie to "Shut the fuck up!"

Having achieved far more than he had envisioned, Mike told the brothers "You'll be seeing me!" and although highly reluctant to do so he turned his back to them and left the bar.

The brothers were staring at the retreating form of Mike, and shared the common thought of "We should just shoot him in the back."

Charlie then lambastes Vinnie "You fuckin idiot, what were you thinking?"

"He doesn't know nothing," Vinnie protested weakly."

Still staring at his sometimes-idiotic younger brother, Charlie pulls his cell phone from his pocket, and flipping it open punches in a number. "Hey you know who this is?" Charlie said to the unfortunate recipient of the call. "You better tell the boss that this cop Chance, is getting to a real pain in the ass.

BLURRED LINE

If he doesn't do something, then we will. Oh, yea that wimp Alfred is starting to get cold feet, and might need a visit as well. I mean it tell the boss, or maybe we will pay you a visit as well." Charlie threatened as he ended the call.

Once again seated in the sanctuary of his car, Mike murmurs to himself "Well Maria, we know who did it, though proving it will be another matter." Mike reaches for his cell phone to advise Larry of these new developments then reluctantly decides not to call until he has irrefutable proof.

Lightly tapping his phone against the steering wheel of his car, completely absorbed in thinking about what his next steps should be Mike felt it begin to buzz with an incoming text message. Seeing the message is from his basketball buddy and fellow Detective Bert Laramie, Mike clicks to open the message. "Hey Mike, B-ball game tonight at Jefferson High School gym, eight o'clock, we'll show those kids how it's done." Grimacing at the remembered painful knees that followed the last game Mike tapped out a quick reply "See you there."

Opening the door to the Gymnasium at Jefferson High School, Mike was greeted by the sounds he loves. The rubber soles of running shoes, squealing in protest at sudden stops and starts on a hardwood floor, accompanying the echo of a bouncing ball. Quickly stripping off his warm up suit, exposing a well-used pair of shorts and T-shirt, Mike changes from his street shoes to his well-used set of running shoes. Joining his team mates for a quick warm up he sizes up the opposing team's young guns. Watching one of the teens approach him Mike remembers him from Miguel's.

"Do you remember me?" asks the gangly teenager

"Yes, you're the waiter at Miguel's." recalling the name tag Mike remembered his name. "Your Tyrone, right?"

"That's right," beamed Tyrone. "My friends call me TJ." he added.

"Ya well don't be tripping me like you did the last game," stated Mike feigning anger.

BLURRED LINE

With an innocent looking shrug of his shoulders TJ replied.
"Hey you tripped over your own feet. I didn't have to trip you."
Winking at Mike, Tyrone quipped. "Don't hurt yourself old
man."

PART TWO

CHAPTER FOURTEEN

Happy Birthday to you. Happy Birthday to you. This
intimate, but extremely boisterous group was performing a lousy
rendition of this song. Tyrone Jackson, more fondly referred to
as TJ, by family and friends, is the recipient of this celebratory
song. TJ surveyed the group of quasi singers. There's Uncle
Glen, he's putting on a brave front as he has just recently lost his
wife of twenty-one years to Sickle Cell Anemia. Uncle George,
who always dominates a room with his bombastic voice and
larger than life persona. Auntie Helen, who claims that TJ,
inherited his ability to play the piano directly from her. Standing
in the corner somewhat removed from the group is his older
brother Mark, although there is three years' difference in age,
Mark and TJ have always been close. TJ has another older
brother named David, but he is unable to attend the festivities
due to the fact he is serving time at the state penitentiary. David
is five years older than TJ, and for the last three years has been a
surrogate father figure to TJ. Finally rounding out the group is
his best friend Ben, watching his friend, TJ smiles realizing that
Ben is lip-syncing the song. TJ was relieved to hear the final run
of Happy Birthdays and begins applauding their effort.

TJ's mom Ophelia, marched proudly into the room bearing a
chocolate cake, at the same time wishing her son a happy
seventeenth birthday.

After the official cake cutting, and everyone declaring that
Ophelia makes the best chocolate cake, the guests soon took
their leave.

BLURRED LINE

With Tyrone and Mark gone off to bed, and the small kitchen cleaned up, Ophelia gratefully sat down at the table. Absently rubbing a tight calf muscle, she thinks about her husband Clive, who chose to miss these family moments. She remembers they started their married life on such a high note, Ophelia thought it was a fairy tale marriage, Clive, handsome and debonair, fresh out of Law School and having successfully passed the State Bar Exam, proudly showed off his license to anyone and everyone. Herself having completed her college degree in office management. They hammered nails into the wall of their third floor one-bedroom apartment, hanging their respective diplomas, laughing at their newly created ego-wall. When David was born, they were ecstatic, as they had both yearned to begin their family with a boy. With the birth of David, they moved into the larger three bed-room ground floor apartment. This seemed palatial compared to what they had lived in, Clive told Ophelia that this was just temporary as he envisioned a detached home in the suburbs. They enjoyed a busy social life attending many fund-raising functions for the under privileged. With the birth of their next two boys Mark, and Tyrone, they decided that their family was complete. As the years sped by they found it a challenge to balance family time against the numerous demands that life places on people. Slowly, and inexorably these pressures grew too great. At first it seemed innocent enough, Clive seemed to enjoy getting photographed with some of his infamous clients. Then he began calling Ophelia late at night, advising her that he would be sleeping at his office due to early morning meetings. At this point in time the boys were becoming upset as they never see their dad, on the rare times he was home he was brusque to the point of being rude to them. All the while his legal practice was expanding exponentially, thus placing even more demands on his time. Ophelia was no longer content to sit at home as the boys were older, so she applied for a position as an office manager for a busy dentist's office.

BLURRED LINE

It was three years ago, now that she caught Clive using drugs in their home, and she quietly issued an ultimatum. "Clive I will not tolerate drugs in this house, it's either myself and your boys, or your drugs, you can't have both. The boys are exposed to enough garbage outside this house without their own father bringing drugs into their home."

Staring at Ophelia for fifteen seconds he announced "Fair enough." He spent ten minutes packing a few clothes then without another word left the house.

At first, she was humiliated and utterly crushed, that he felt so little for her and the boys that it took only a few heartbeats for him to decide. Then the anger set in and after a few heartfelt expletives directed at Clive, mentally gathered herself for the forthcoming challenges of being both parents to three boys.

Not willing to cast any aspersions on their father despite his apparent eagerness to leave, Ophelia attempted to explain to the boys that his leaving was a mutually agreed upon decision. She bore the brunt of their anger and resentment for the next six months.

One afternoon arriving home from school TJ was surprised to see his mom home before him. "Hey Mom" bending down to kiss her cheek on his way to the fridge. "How come you're already home from the office?" opening the fridge and surveying the contents.

Ophelia lovingly admonished her youngest son stating "Tyrone that is refrigerator not an air conditioner."

"Your right mom," grabbing a juice box closes the fridge. "So why are you home early?" reiterating his question knowing that his mom rarely takes time off from her job.

Shuffling items in her purse she informed him that its parent/teacher interviews at his school.

"Cool," replied TJ.

"You don't sound concerned."

"No mom, it's all good," he responded confidently sitting down at the kitchen table.

BLURRED LINE

Fondly watching his mom dig in her purse he remarked. "If you had a smaller purse you might actually find whatever it is you're looking for."

"No need to get smart young man," she quips with an equally fond glance at her son.

Observing his mom, he was dismayed to see that this lady of five feet two inches, with a slim build is beginning to get gray hair. He finds it disconcerting to realize that she is beginning to show signs of aging.

"What did I do with those house keys?" Ophelia wondered out loud after unsuccessfully locating them in her cavernous purse.

"I thought I saw them on the table by the door."

"Oh, okay thanks son," rising from the table she asked TJ if he has to go to work today.

"No, Arnold gave me the afternoon off I'm just going to hang out here."

"See you shortly," his mom called leaving for her appointed meetings with TJ's teachers.

With TJ being in grade twelve, and teetering on the brink of adulthood, he is asking himself what he would like to do. He is painfully aware that his lanky five foot ten-inch frame will not garner any attention from basketball scouts. He has loved playing the game since he was old enough to bounce a ball. His friends often say they hear TJ's ball bouncing off the pavement before they see him. Knowing that lacking the financial assistance a college basketball scholarship would bring, attending even a state college will not be in his future. He also realizes that though he excels at playing the piano without the benefit of formal training, he certainly does not see himself becoming a concert pianist. Stretched out on the couch watching television and dozing, TJ heard the outside door open, then close thinking it was his brother arriving home from work, he once again closed his eyes. When he heard, his mom call his name he was surprised to find that two hours had slipped by.

"Tyrone, can you come into the kitchen please?"

BLURRED LINE

Entering the kitchen and leaning up against the counter, he attempted to discern his mother's mood with a discreet look at her face.

"Well Tyrone, the teachers are all in agreement that you're well-liked and respected among your peers. They also feel that you have the potential to be on the honor roll, and even class president, I'm very proud of you son, but I wonder why you aren't. This is the year you graduate from High School and choose a career, who knows what doors might open for you if you were class valedictorian," she concluded with obvious pride in her voice.

Staring thoughtfully at his mom TJ quietly asked her. "Where would you hide a tree mom?"

"For goodness sake's Tyrone, we're not talking about trees."

"No mom, where would you hide a tree?" TJ quietly insisted.

Looking quizzically at her son, Ophelia thinks about it for a minute then with a triumphant smile declares. "I would hide a tree in a forest."

"That's right mom, and that is exactly what I'm doing, the last thing I want to do is bring attention to myself, as not all attention is a good thing. You remember that Mark Levine guy? He was class valedictorian, and the teachers told everyone that he would one day write a great book. When he was interviewed by the Daily Sentinel, he advised them he was going to write a book on the criminal element in the city, more importantly he wanted to expose the rogue cop whose rumored to control a group of enforcers. Mark ended up in the hospital with two broken legs, and a mangled writing hand. I'm pretty sure he's not gonna write any books," finished TJ.

"Going to" Tyrone "Not gonna," his mom gently corrected him.

CHAPTER FIFTEEN

TJ, has been best friends with Ben Harris since they were both in grade four, they didn't start out on friendly terms. They both had a crush on the same girl, so they figured they should go to a deserted alley after school one day, and settle this dispute. After giving each other a bloody nose, they decided the issue was settled and became best friends, funny thing is they both forgot about the girl.

Over the years growing up, TJ and Ben have had their share of back alley scraps with other boys.

Ben would laugh at TJ stating. "Good thing you don't plan on becoming a boxer as you can't fight your way out of a wet paper bag."

TJ agreed wholeheartedly with this synopsis. They have both refused to become affiliated with a local street gang, this action has caused them to become outcasts with some members of their peer group.

The two friends have started considering their futures, and what they want to do upon graduation from high school, they share a mutual yearning to travel.

Ben had commented. "Well if we join the army we would likely get to travel."

TJ remains non-committal with this idea, not sure if a career in the army would be right for him.

Laughing and clapping TJ on the shoulder, Ben exclaimed. "We could be the new poster boys for the army."

"Well I certainly could with my good looks, but there's no way in hell you're going to be on the poster," replied TJ with a wry smile.

BLURRED LINE

Howling with laughter and holding his sides in mock pain, Ben pointed at his buddy sputtering. "You the poster boy!"

It is moments like this that TJ realizes how highly he values his friendship with Ben

"So, who are you going to invite to the prom next month?" Ben enquired of TJ.

"I think that I would like to ask Conchita, lately we have been talking quite a bit at the restaurant."

"Oh, that's right, her dad Arnold owns Miguel's."

"What about you buddy?"

Suddenly feeling a completely unexpected urge to divulge a long-held secret, Ben took a gamble. "We have been friends practically all our lives TJ, I have been waiting a long time to bring this up. I won't be asking a girl to the prom, I'm going to ask Bill." though terrified of what TJ's reaction might be, Ben stared at him attempting to gauge his reaction.

Reaching out and placing his hand on his friend's shoulder, TJ squeezed gently. "I have always thought that you might be gay, I can't explain why I felt that as you have certainly been successful at disguising your feelings. It has never affected the way I feel about you, and it never will buddy."

Unable to control the tears slowly rolling down his cheeks. Ben asked TJ why he never said anything.

Shrugging his shoulders, TJ replied. "It was none of my business to say anything. I figured if you wanted me to know you would tell me. You being gay, or straight, is not important to me, what's important to me, is you being my friend."

"Thank-you for that TJ, you're the first person I have told."

"Your parents don't know?"

"I think mom suspects something but I think she is scared to talk to me about it."

"When did you start to think, you might be gay?

BLURRED LINE

Attempting to quell the anger he felt at the question, Ben fired a question right back at TJ. 'When did you know, you were straight?"

"Never much thought about it, just doing what comes naturally I guess." replied a thoughtful TJ.

"So why can't the same rule apply to me? Why does the world consider gay's to be unnatural, when all we are doing is following our instincts? It's not like I ate a rotten tomato one day and woke up gay the next. I am no different than you buddy I'm just following my instincts."

Holding up his hands in a defensive posture TJ declared. "Whoa Ben, I said I don't have a problem at all with you being gay. You don't have to get pissed at me, in fact, I admire your courage inviting Bill to the prom, that won't be easy. This Bill your talking about that's not Bill Rapachek is it? No matter, you are stuck with me as your best friend."

"Jesus ya sorry about that. It's like I was talking to my mom and trying to explain it to her." apologized Ben. "Yes, it is Bill Rapachek," he affirms.

On a sunny Wednesday afternoon as they walked to their respective jobs, TJ feels that something is bothering his friend and asks him about it.

"You remember when I was sick last winter, my dad doesn't have any medical insurance, so he borrowed some money to pay for my treatment. Dad couldn't go to a bank to get the money, so he borrowed it from some loan shark. I guess they haven't been paying it back, and now they are threatening my parents. Mom is worried about what might happen if they can't pay it back."

"Jesus Christ, that really sucks," muttered TJ. "So, what are they going to do?"

"Not sure," replied a worried looking Ben. "Mom has been saying we should move to where her brother lives, it might be safer there."

BLURRED LINE

While TJ absorbs what, his friend has said, he wonders if introducing Ben to that cop he has played Basketball against would help. Mentally kicking himself TJ mused *"just because he plays basketball doesn't mean he's a good cop."* Everyone on the street knows half the cops in the city are on the take, there is widespread cynicism regarding the honesty of the police force among the citizens of Metro-City.

Approaching Lee's Groceries Store, where Ben works as a stock boy, Ben spots his boss Jimmie out on the sidewalk talking on his cell phone.

Ben whispered to TJ. "Watch what Jimmie does when I bump him".

Watching Ben bump Jimmie as he walked by, TJ laughed as Jimmie inconspicuously attempted to straighten his bad toupee, whilst at the same time shout at Ben. "Why you always bump me?"

In a somewhat lighter mood, TJ waves to Ben as he continues walking the three blocks to his job as a waiter at Miguel's restaurant.

CHAPTER SIXTEEN

The day TJ's world turned upside down started out like any other school day. His mom calling him three times, before finally threatening to enter his bedroom with a bucket of cold water to throw on him.

When TJ finally arrived in the kitchen, he gave his mom a peck on the cheek remarking, "Since they don't own a bucket she would be unable to carry out her threat."

"Don't be smart young man" mildly rebuked a smiling Ophelia. "Never underestimate a mother's ingenuity. So, what would you like for breakfast?"

"Cereals good."

"Any plans for after school today?"

"No, nothing special, Arnold gave me the day off so I might play some three on three basketball with Ben and some friends."

"Okay just remember it's a school night so don't be late. I must go to Auntie Helen's after work, there's soup in the cupboard, or make a grilled cheese for supper."

Putting his bowl in the sink, TJ glanced at the clock and remarked. "I better get going Ben will be here shortly." calling out. "See you later mom." as he grabs his basketball and heads for the door.

"Don't slam the door," she yelled to no avail as the walls tremor from the force of the door closing.

As TJ navigates his way through another boring day at school, he decides that he should ask Conchita next week about the prom. He can only hope that she will accept as there is no one else he would like to ask. A midst all the jostling in the crowded noisy hallway on his way to his third period class, TJ feels someone grab his bicep.

BLURRED LINE

Looking at the owner of the offending hand TJ was surprised to see it's Conchita. Feeling himself being towed against the current towards a small sanctuary against a row of lockers, TJ went willingly.

"So, mister when the hell are you going to ask me to the prom?" demanded the beautiful Conchita. "I have already told some friends that you asked me to go as your date."

Drinking in Conchita's beauty, TJ was temporarily at a loss for words. The long black hair, the dark brown eyes which he finds himself lost in.

"You were going to ask me, weren't you?"

"Of course," stammered TJ. Then deciding that he needed to display his courage, formally asked Conchita if she would be his date for prom. He was ecstatic when she agrees to this.

"Are you working tonight?" she asks TJ.

"Uh no, your dad gave the afternoon off."

"Well since you won't be there tonight I will do it now," she then kissed TJ on the lips, and rushed off disappearing in the still crowded hallway.

In a complete fog, TJ walks unseeing past his destination. Realizing he has missed his room, he quickly back tracks and gains the refuge of his seat. He can't help grinning like the village idiot as he replays the last five minutes of his life. Thinking to himself. "That *didn't hurt at all.*" The remainder of the school day literally flew by.

Sitting on the small front stoop of their apartment that afternoon, TJ is absently bouncing his ball waiting for Ben. TJ's reverie is snapped when he hears Ben call his name. he wants to tell Ben what had transpired with Conchita, but decides that after Ben's revelation he might wait.

As they make their way to the Jeffers's Street basketball court, Ben has a surprise for TJ.

"Hey hope you don't mind TJ, but Bill will be our third player."

"Is he any good?"

"Ya he's not bad."

BLURRED LINE

"Then I don't mind at all."
"Holy Shit." Ben gasped slumping on the bench at half time. "I'm so out of shape "he declares as sweat pours off him. Grabbing his water bottle and gulping down the refreshment, TJ is somewhat amused to hear Bill caution Ben about consuming too much too quickly.

"Hey come on you pansies. We're just getting started with you," taunted their opponents.

An hour later TJ taunted their opponents "Who's the pansies now?" jeered TJ as they vanquished their opponents four games to two.

"Hey TJ, Bill and I were going to grab a burger want to join us?"

Although his stomach is rumbling a protest at the lack of food coming its way, TJ declines the offer. He decides that he should head home as he has some school work to get done. Arriving at the intersection of Jeffer's and Lincoln, he thinks about which way he should go. If he takes Jeffer's he will be home quicker, but that would mean going by Jo's Bar and Grill and it will be dark by then. This is a place best avoided if possible, his stomach made the decision for him, and bouncing his ball heads down Jeffer's.

As TJ is about to pass Jo's he hears the unmistakable sounds of bare fists hitting flesh, accompanied by low grunts of pain. TJ froze, as he considers his options on how best to avoid detection, it is already so dark that he can barely make out the figures. Then thinking that he should be able to sneak through the back alley slowly begins to backtrack. TJ had only just entered his escape route when to his utter dismay, he sees two men drag a third man into the alley. Quickly finding refuge behind some wooden boxes in the debris strewn ally, TJ can only listen helplessly as the beating continues.

Peering around the boxes to see what is happening, TJ is horrified to see one of the figures point a gun at the kneeling victim.

BLURRED LINE

He heard the guy pointing the gun, say to the victim. "You had your chance and you blew it, so now it's time to pay the piper." and without further ado casually shot the victim in the head. Having now witnessed a murder, TJ knows that he needs to extricate himself from this area immediately.

Taking a step backwards in the dark, he did not notice a steel pipe balanced precariously against the boxes. It toppled over with what seemed like an ear shattering clang, TJ froze, closing his eyes against the forlorn hope that they did not hear it. That wishful thought was dashed when he heard one of them shout.

"Go check out that noise Vinnie, I will get the car."

"Hey enough with the names already Charlie," growled the one called Vinnie. "Never know who might be listening." Grumbling about having to go see what was likely some stray mutt scrounging a meal, Vinnie heads to investigate the noise.

As TJ hears Vinnie approaching, the fear he is feeling manifests itself in beads of sweat running off his brow. When Vinnie gets within a mere ten feet of TJ's hiding spot, TJ acts without conscious thought. Stepping out from behind his refuge, TJ drew a bead on Vinnie's face, then threw his basketball harder than he has ever done before. He was instantly rewarded when he sees it land squarely on the nose of the unsuspecting Vinnie.

"Son of Bitch!" hollered the injured Vinnie as he dropped to his knees, cupping his hands around his injured nose. "Jesus Christ," he moaned as tears from his eyes join the river of blood issuing from his nose.

Meanwhile, TJ has left the scene running faster than he ever has before in his young life, knowing full well the consequences if he is caught. He has only one thought in his mind and that is to gain the sanctuary of his home as soon as possible. It seems in no time at all TJ arrives at his front door, digging in his pocket for the apartment key.

Once inside the apartment, TJ slammed the door shut and with a huge exhalation leans against the door. Pushing off from the door TJ heads to the kitchen table on legs that feel like rubber.

BLURRED LINE

Slumping down in a chair, cradling his head in his hands, TJ emits a low groan lurches up and dashes for the bathroom. He barely makes it to the toilet when he begins to violently retch. Feeling completely drained he leans against the bathroom wall and with elbows against his knees rests his head on joined hands, while regaining his equilibrium. He is about to call out for his mom when he remembers she was going to Auntie Helen's. Regaining his feet, TJ turns on the tap in the sink and bending over rinses the foul-tasting saliva from his mouth. Heading to his bedroom TJ removes his sweat soaked shirt and throws it into the clothes hamper, replacing it with a clean one. Falling onto his bed his mind replayed what he witnessed, and he knew that he is in serious trouble. Several times he is tempted to call Ben, and tell him what has happened but decides that if he does his friend may up in the same predicament. TJ mentally scolds himself. *What an idiot you are, if you had just gone with Ben this wouldn't have happened.* Surprisingly enough, TJ's eyes close and dozes off. Hearing the outside door close, TJ is instantly awake and the reality of his situation came rushing back.

Making his way to the kitchen, TJ sees his brother Mark bent over looking in the open fridge.

Closing the fridge door and turning, Mark glanced at his younger brother TJ exclaiming. "Man, you look like shit, what happened?" Mark is both surprised and alarmed to see tears roll down his brother's cheeks.

"I'm in big trouble Mark," murmured TJ. TJ then relays the details of what has transpired. Only once does Mark interrupt.

"What were those names you heard?".

"Vinnie and Charlie."

"Shit, I was afraid those were the names you said."

"Why," asks TJ

"If it's who I think it is, they would be the Delveccio brothers. They are two of the worst criminals in the city."

"Fuckin Great," moaned TJ.

"Did they see you?"

BLURRED LINE

"I don't think so," responded TJ, smiling at the vision of Vinnie catching his basketball with his nose adds. "I'm pretty sure Vinnie didn't."

"Where's your ball?"

"Not sure, after I hit Vinnie with it I was kind of busy running for my life."

"Hmm, does your ball have your name on it? Or anything that would identify you as the owner?"

"Not really," answered TJ then added "Pretty much everyone knows my ball though."

"Well we will deal with that when we have to I guess."

"Shouldn't we call the police?" asked a subdued TJ

Mark continues to stare at the table apparently lost in thought. "What did you say TJ?"

"Shouldn't we call the police.? There is that cop that I play basketball against he seems alright."

Mark replies emphatically "No, we don't know who we can trust. Unfortunately, that guy is already in a place where he won't be found. The Delveccio's will deny everything, and they would now know who you are. So, that is not an option, Mark then begins to lay out his plan to TJ. "From this moment on you are sick in bed. You will talk to no one, not even Ben. I will call Miguel's and tell them you won't be in due to illness. Most importantly you will not say anything to mom about this, she will want to call the cops and that could be disastrous. We won't worry about your ball right now, for all we know it may never be found, or maybe some kid will just pick it up and take it home. So off to bed TJ before mom gets home." commanded Mark. "And stay there until I get back."

"Back from where?" asked TJ

"I will be seeing and talking to some people about this, and I might be gone a couple of days." he replied in a calmer voice now that he has a tentative plan that may save his brother's life.

"Mark, I can't thank you enough for helping me out of this mess."

BLURRED LINE

"Don't thank me just yet, we have a long way to go to get clear of this."

As TJ follows his brother's dictates and heads to bed, he is relieved that Mark is taking control. Setting his alarm to wake him an hour before his mom gets up TJ has a plan of his own that will convince his mom he's sick.

CHAPTER SEVENTEEN

Reaching over and slapping his alarm clock into silence, TJ's head falls back onto his pillow, wondering what his brother will come up with to extricate him from this mess.

Then rising from his bed, he begins to implement his own plan, walking to the bathroom he locates the hot water bottle. Turning on the hot water tap, he allows it to run till there is steam visibly rising from the water. Filling the hot water bottle, he then heads back to his room and bed, placing the water bottle on his head TJ yelped in pain as it is hot enough to burn. Not willing to give up his plan just yet, he decides to hold the bottle close to his forehead. Right on time at seven a.m., his mom knocks on his door telling him it's time to get up. "Mom I think I have the flu," moaned TJ.

Marching into TJ's room, and placing her hands on her hips Ophelia asks. "Do you have an exam today that you never studied for, because you're never sick?"

"No mom, I think I have a fever feel my forehead," moaned TJ

Indulging her son Ophelia walks over and places the back of her hand on his forehead. "Mm, yes you feel warm alright son, you might have something, just not sure what."

"See mom I was right, I do have the flu," declared TJ.

As Ophelia turned to leave the bedroom she comments. "Well son, since you're so obviously ill you should stay in bed all day. You probably should not eat anything either, but drink lots of water that may flush out whatever it is you have. Oh and by the way, please don't forget to put the hot water bottle back where you found it."

"But mom," protested TJ

BLURRED LINE

"Don't but mom, me young man, the lines from the bottle are visible on your forehead. Perhaps it was too hot to start with, I'm not sure why you want to stay home today, I can only assume you are unprepared for an exam." Waving a finger at her son she warns him he better not fails any courses. Feeling dejected that he was unable to even fool his mom, TJ wonders how in the hell his life has gone so awry, in just twenty-four hours. Deciding that he might as well get up, he empties the hot water bottle and returns it. At the same time gently rubbing the tender spot on his forehead muttering, "Fuckin thing." Feeling somewhat better after a shower and eating some toast slathered in peanut butter and jam, TJ hits the couch to play some video games. Hearing the phone ring, TJ thinking it's his mom calling to check on him slowly walks over to answer it. He is surprised to hear his brother Mark's voice.

"Hey TJ how you doing?"

"Alright so far I guess. How long am I going to be stuck in the house?" asked the despondent TJ

"Not long bud, I'll be home tonight."

"Good, not sure how long I can do this stuck in the house thing."

"Well TJ, you may not like the alternative." Mark reluctantly states. "Go to my bedroom closet and my old suitcase should be there. Pack some clothes and whatever you might need for a bit of a holiday."

"I have to leave home?" exclaimed TJ

"I'll explain when I get home, just do what I said TJ." requested Mark as he ends the call.

"What the fuck?" TJ exclaims loudly to the empty apartment. No sooner had he headed to Mark's room to retrieve the suitcase, when he heard the shrill ringing of the phone.

"Phone never quits ringing." TJ mutters as turns back to answer it, and once again expecting to hear his mother's voice.

"TJ is that you?" asked his oldest brother David.

A completely surprised TJ stammered. "David?"

BLURRED LINE

"Ya it's me kiddo. Don't say anything, just let me talk as you never know who else might be listening. Mark was here and told me about your problem. We have decided that you will need to leave for a while, we know it sucks but for now it's all we can do. I wanted to call to let you know that Mark and myself have considered all the options, and this one might be best. So, do what Mark says and hopefully we can get you through this. Love you TJ, I really miss out times together goodbye."

In a daze, TJ once again heads to Mark's bedroom to retrieve the suitcase, he is now beginning to get mad as it seems he has lost all control of his immediate future. Having never really felt anger before, he is surprised at the rage he is feeling over this turn of events. Tossing the decrepit looking suitcase onto his bed, he wonders why the fuck he must leave. He had the misfortune to witness two lowlifes execute some poor son of a bitch, and he must leave. If he could only remember that cops name, he would call and tell him everything that happened, then he would not have to leave. He feels that by leaving he is running away, and those two Delveccio's get away with murder.

Sitting down for supper with Tyrone, Ophelia watches him as he listlessly pushes his food around the plate. This is out of character, for someone whose food usually disappears like it was sucked up by a vacuum

"Still not feeling well son?" she asks with concern evident in her voice.

"No, I'm not," answered a despondent TJ.

"Auntie Helen asked me to go shopping with her tonight. If you would rather I stay home with you I will."

"No, I'll be alright, you go."

"Hey where is Mark?" wondered Ophelia out loud. "It's not like him to miss supper."

Shrugging his shoulders TJ mutters. "Ya don't know."

Hearing a loud knocking on the door causes TJ to jump as he is not expecting anyone.

BLURRED LINE

"Could you get that please son, it's likely Auntie Helen here to pick me up."

Answering the door TJ grunts what passes for a hello to his not so favorite Aunt. The shrill ringing of the phone saves him from having any further conversation with her. Answering the phone, TJ waves to his mom as she leaves with her sister.

"Hello?"

"Hey TJ it's Ben. Where were you today?"

Remembering Mark's cautionary words about telling anyone TJ sticks to the story line. "Ya must have caught a bug, felt pretty shitty all day. So I stayed home."

Without preamble Ben, glumly states. "My dad has left us, they had a huge fight the other night and he left."

"Jesus Christ, that sucks," replied TJ instantly remembering how he felt when his own dad left.

"He never even said goodbye."

TJ remembers the feeling, his own dad leaving without a word. The feeling that his dad never cared for him still lingers painfully, his mom tried to explain that his dad loved him, but TJ was not buying it. If he cared for me at all he would said something TJ had protested.

"Hey you still there?" asked Ben.

"Sorry Bud was thinking about what you said," explained TJ

"I was asking if I could come over for a bit?"

"Oh, man I wish you could, but mom thinks I'm playing Jack. She thinks I didn't want to do a test at school, so I'm kind of grounded," TJ is disgusted with himself at having to lie to his friend.

"Okay Bud, see you at school then," concluded a distraught Ben. Not having heard his brother Mark arrive home. TJ is surprised to see him enter the kitchen.

"Who was on the phone?"

"Just Ben." answered TJ adding. "His dad has left them."

"Hmm seems all dads do that. Have kids then fuckin leave.

BLURRED LINE

Grab a chair TJ, and I will tell you what David and I came up
with. Speaking bluntly Mark then laid out the plan. "We think
you should go to South -Bend."

Not comprehending what Mark was saying, TJ was about to ask
when Mark holding up a hand stated. "Wait till I finish, David
says our poor excuse for a father has a half-brother there.
According to what dad told David a long time ago, this guy was
in the special forces. His name is Jebidiah Walker, his wife died
a few years ago, and he is pretty much a recluse."

At this point in time TJ loses the slim hold he has on his temper
and explodes. "Why the hell do I have to go to a place I've never
heard of and stay with someone I've never met?" Who in the hell
is Jebidiah Walker?"

"I just told you, weren't you listening?" Mark answered calmly
in the face of TJ's outburst. Then continuing as though there was
no interruption. "He has a small farm about thirty minutes out of
South -Bend, no one knows he is related to us. David thinks
mom met him once, other than that no one here knows of him."

"What about dad?" asked TJ

"What about him?" grunted Mark

"Maybe he could help."

"Shit TJ, he can't help himself. I guess mom hasn't told you,
his office is deserted, he just packed up and left. He couldn't
even let his family know, we found out through one of his
clients."

Staring at his brother, not wanting to believe his dad would do
this, TJ was heartbroken.

"So, what would happen if I didn't go to this South -Bend
place?" asked a dejected TJ.

"Quite likely the Delveccio's would discover that you are the
one who witnessed the killing and they would see to it you never
tell anyone. In fact, I have heard from a guy that the two brothers
have sworn out a complaint to the police. The police are going to
investigate an unprovoked attack on Vinnie, they are now
searching for this unknown perpetrator.

BLURRED LINE

"Are you kidding me?" howled an indignant TJ. "They killed a guy, and they swear out a complaint against me," shaking his head in absolute disbelief.

"Ya well remember it's not like the Delveccio's are gonna tell the cops they killed someone. All the cops know is Vinnie shows up with a spectacularly smashed nose, which he claims is from an unprovoked attack. Now not only are the brother's looking for you, they have the cops looking as well."

"Shit," muttered TJ.

"When I was with David we called Jebidiah, we told him that you have to get out of town for a while due to girl trouble. He was not necessarily happy to hear from us. In fact, he seems to be a miserable bastard. But since we're family, he was willing to take you in, you can help him with chores and he won't charge you for grub."

"What the fuck is grub?" asked a bewildered TJ.

Smiling across the table at his brother Mark answers. "I think it's food."

Resigning himself to the fact that to stay out of reach of the Delveccio brothers, he must go to South -Bend and stay with some miserable bastard that eats grub. "When will I have to leave?"

"There is a bus leaving in a couple of hours. When you get there just to be on the safe side don't use your real name. You will have seven hours on the bus to think of a new name."

At this point in time TJ is overwhelmed and unleashes a barrage of questions at his brother. "What are you going to tell Mom? Can I call Ben? How long will I have to be gone for?"

"Don't worry about mom, David is going to call her and explain everything to her. David and I wish we could tell you how long you might be gone, but right now we just don't know.

BLURRED LINE

As far as Ben goes, yes call him, but tell him you must go help an Uncle, just be very careful not to say where he lives," concluded a somber Mark.

Entering the only bedroom, he has known in his short seventeen years, TJ slowly looks around as if attempting to memorize every detail. Grabbing the decrepit suitcase in one hand, and with one last look he turns off the light and closing the door, thinking that this chapter in his life might be over. During the short twenty-minute ride to the bus station both Mark and TJ are very quiet. Each immersed in their own thoughts, they would not be surprised to know they were both wondering when they would see each other again. When TJ is about to board his bus, Mark thrusts a handful of money at him, and gives him a hug. TJ notices that the tears flowing from his brother's eyes mirror his own.

CHAPTER EIGHTEEN

As daylight begins to chase away the remaining vestiges of shadows from the night time hours, TJ rests his forehead against the cool glass of the window. A sign flashes by mercifully announcing South -Bend to be only ten miles away. To TJ, the bus trip has been an excruciatingly long, mind numbing trip. His sense of adventure is slowly winning the war against the trepidation he is feeling about the unknown. Being so accustomed to the congestion of the city, TJ is amazed to see such large expanses of unoccupied area. Feeling the motion of the bus begin to change minutely, TJ begins to see houses dotting the landscape. Then without warning the bus comes to an abrupt halt, a midst the noisy exhalation of air brakes being applied. The driver stands up, stretches, and proclaims to the half empty, and mostly uncaring passengers that they have arrived in South- Bend. As TJ rose from his seat, he feels his pants plastered to his buttocks, putting his hand to the back of his pants he surreptitiously pulls the offending material away. Making his way to the front of the bus and disembarking, TJ spots the driver with his head stuck in the luggage compartment.

"You only had the one bag, right?" enquired the driver.

"Yes. Am I the only one getting off here?" asked the bleary-eyed TJ.

With a clearly exaggerated motion, the driver looks around and declares sarcastically. "Yep looks like you're the only one getting off," chuckling at his own wit the driver slams the luggage compartment door closed then without another glance at TJ re-boards the bus.

As the forlorn TJ watches, the bus begins to slowly move away leaving in its wake a cloud of noxious exhaust fumes.

BLURRED LINE

Spending seven hours confined to the stale, warm air in the bus, TJ now dons his hoodie to fend off the chill of the early morning air. TJ is alarmed as he realizes there is absolutely no one around. No Uncle Jebidiah, no one even walking on the sidewalk, the only thing moving is a three-legged dog across the street that temporarily stopped his foraging to stare at TJ. Grasping the handle of his suitcase, TJ decides to see if there is a restaurant or coffee shop open as he is famished.

After a short walk, he is rewarded when he sees a neon sign declaring that Nina's coffee shop is open. Upon entering TJ notices about a dozen diners scattered randomly throughout the booths with a few also seated at the counter. Hearing the noisy tinkle of the bell atop the entryway, all but one of the patrons turn to stare at TJ. Feeling like an intruder TJ quickly finds refuge in a deserted booth, removing himself from the probing stares of the early morning diners. No sooner is he seated when he is approached by a short stocky lady, TJ finds his eyes drawn to the bright red hair which is clearly in a state of disarray.

"Good morning, and how are you today young man?" she asked in a soft lilting tone of voice with just a trace of an accent.

"Hi there, actually I'm kind of hungry," stammered TJ.

With a smile that can only be described as contagious she carries on with. "I know, I bet you just came in on the bus."

Returning the smile. TJ asks her how she guessed he just came into town on the bus.

"I'm Nina and I have owned this place for ten years now, I pretty much know everyone in town. As you can tell when you walked in strangers are very noticeable here."

"Ya sort of noticed that alright," agreed TJ.

"So, if you're hungry, I would recommend the Ranch-hands breakfast, most everyone around here orders that."

"Okay, thank-you."

Watching as she disappears into the bowel of her kitchen, TJ becomes aware that the ebb and flow of conversation between the early morning diners has once again resumed.

BLURRED LINE

In no time at all she was back with a large glass of orange juice, as well as a plate that held a stack of pancakes, two fried eggs and bacon.

"I'll be right back," she promised.

Looking at the food piled on the plate, TJ is amazed that it all stayed on the plate. Picking up his knife and fork, the famished TJ begins to make the food disappear. Barely glancing up from his task, he senses that Nina has returned. Raising his head to look at her TJ is a little embarrassed at the way he has been devouring the food.

"Don't mind me," said Nina. "I'm used to seeing people with healthy appetites eat."

Pointing at his plate TJ exclaims. "This is very good!"

"Thank-you for the compliment, so if you don't mind me asking, since you know my name what can I call you?"

TJ almost forgets that he shouldn't use his real name and thinking quickly replies "JT".

"Okay JT, I really hope you don't mind me asking questions. It's just unusual to see a young man such as yourself traveling alone."

Putting down his knife and fork and taking along drink of orange juice to buy himself some time, TJ then explains that he is here to visit his uncle, Jebidiah Walker.

Staring at TJ with a puzzled look on her face, she covered the moment with. "Well there you go JT; I never knew Jeb had any family at all. We used to see him and his wife Patricia in here regularly, but ever since she passed away Jeb has become a recluse." Hearing her name called Nina excuses herself and heads back to work. TJ in the meantime has once again attacked the single remaining pancake on his plate, then in a vain attempt at stifling a stentorian sounding belch, covers his mouth with his hand. TJ observes the one guy who never turned to face the door when he entered the diner, approach his table.

BLURRED LINE

"Hi their son, mind if I sit down?" Not waiting for TJ to answer
he proceeds to sit down anyways. "Allow me to introduce
myself. I'm Larry Donovan, Chief of Police for South -Bend."

Although the name meant nothing to TJ, the face sure did.
Feigning dis-interest in the hopes of masking any visible signs of
recognition JT simply replies. "Oh Ya."

Sounding somewhat skeptical Larry states. "Nina tells me your
name is JT and you're Jebidiah Walker's nephew, also you're
here to visit him for a while."

"That's right I am, he was supposed to pick me up at the bus
stop, not sure what happened, maybe he forgot."

"Tell you what, if you don't mind waiting a couple of hours I
can give you a lift out there."

Sensing that Larry for some reason does not believe he is
Jeb's nephew and has offered the ride to ensure that is where he
is going, TJ reluctantly agreed.

Rising from the table TJ begins heading to the cashier to pay
for his breakfast, when Larry once again speaks up.

"Since you are going to be staying at old Jebs, this is quite
likely the last decent meal you are going to enjoy for a while so
allow me to pay for it." As they are about to exit the diner Larry
yells into the general area of the kitchen. "Hey Nina put JT's
breakfast on my tab please."

Amid the clatter and banging of pots they hear Nina
acknowledge Larry's request. Standing outside, the diner Larry
invites JT to do some sightseeing, and not to worry Larry will
find him when he's able to run him out to Jebs place. Watching
Larry descend from the slightly raised sidewalk JT breathed a
sigh of relief at not being recognized. He is positive that this
Larry is the cop who was arguing with his partner in Miguel's.
He remembers thinking at the time that if those two big cops got
into it they would demolish the restaurant. "Shit." he muttered to
himself. Of all places for that cop to be. Then remembering that
Larry was the only one who never turned around when he
entered the diner, JT slips back into Nina's.

BLURRED LINE

Walking furtively towards where he thinks Larry was sitting at the counter, JT suddenly sees his reflection. Tucked inconspicuously among the glasses on the shelf is a little mirror that affords an uninterrupted view of the doorway. Seeing Nina emerge from the kitchen TJ tells her that he thought he forgot his wallet, then quickly leaves the diner.

CHAPTER NINETEEN

South -Bend is a quiet town of some seventeen hundred souls, situated between rolling hills and grassy flat lands. The river from which the towns name is derived from, flows slowly and nonchalantly just east of town. This is the type of town that until your family has resided here for three generations you are classed as newcomers. There is an elementary school, as well as a combined middle/ high school. There is a local paper called the South -Bend Crier, that is published bi-monthly. The owner and sole reporter John Finkelstein, dreams of one day writing a story worthy of a Pulitzer prize.

The South -Bend town council consists of five well-meaning citizens. Mayor Ralph Hoskins, winning the previous four civic elections by acclamation, and will likely win the next four the same way. Ralph is your typical hale and hearty politician, always back slapping and shaking hands as though there were an election the following week. He remains blissfully unaware that his position as Mayor is quite safe, for the simple reason no one else wants the job.

Mary-Anne Whitley, who due to advanced age finds it a challenge to remain awake during council meetings. Dan Jones is the mover and shaker on council, his personal quest is to lure big box stores to South -Bend. Hank Jones has been a counselor for as long as his first cousin Dan. Rounding out the council is John Brock; his family has only resided in South -Bend for two generations. It's widely thought that he represents the new comers to town.

BLURRED LINE

The Police force in South -Bend, consists of two full time constables. "Wiley Willy" Jones who also just happens to be Dan and Hanks favorite nephew. Willy earned the nick name by apprehending South -Bend's most notorious shop lifter.

As a teenager growing up in South -Bend, Willy was never able to gain the respect of his peers. He was much taller than his classmates, and due to tough economic times his parents could only afford pants that were perennially four inches too short. It came as no surprise to anyone that Willy became a police officer to gain the respect he so desperately sought.

Completing the roster is Irene Ingalls, what Irene lacks in stature she more than compensates for in her drive to be a successful police constable. She has faithfully served the citizens of South -Bend for a period of four years now. When the office of Police Chief was unexpectedly available due to the sudden passing of Samuel Hoskins, Irene promptly applied. She lobbied long and hard for this position, oblivious to the fact Mayor Hoskins already had a candidate in mind.

Mayor Hoskins, was both pleased and pleasantly surprised that it took only one phone call to lure Larry Donovan back to South -Bend as the new Police Chief. He had, through business associates in Metro- City followed Larry's career. He was aware of the troubles Larry had with his father as a teenager, and was troubled by the fact that the late Sam Hoskins failed to arrest Larry's father for child abuse.

In the brief two months, that Larry has been Chief of Police, Willy Jones has developed a hero worship attitude towards Larry. Willy feels that by standing close to Larry perhaps some of the respect afforded Larry, will rub off on him. Irene on the other hand is barely civil towards the new chief. She is resentful that she was not awarded the position and at times her attitude borders on insubordination.

CHAPTER TWENTY

With a full stomach and his sense of trepidation on the ebb, TJ
picks up his suitcase and begins walking along the sidewalk. His
concerns regarding the cop recognizing him have also subsided.
He is puzzled though as to how that cop from the city is now the
Police Chief here. Walking along the sidewalk TJ hears a
peculiar clicking sound emanating from behind him, turning he
sees the three-legged dog about five steps behind him. At first,
he is slightly alarmed the dog may be aggressive, but the
wagging tail seemed to indicate otherwise. Turning back in the
direction he was headed he notices across the street a store called
The Mercantile. Never having been in a Mercantile before, TJ
crosses the street and enters the store. He is amazed at the many
items for sale, it seems everything from horse saddles to kitchen
sinks are available. Strolling down an isle he spots a magazine
and book rack. Noticing the latest edition of his favorite
basketball magazine, he is soon completely immersed in the
stories. It was only when he felt his arm bumped that he became
aware of someone else beside him.

"Well, please excuse my clumsiness young man, and allow me
to introduce myself. My name is Robert Lane."

"No problem," replied TJ.

Looking carefully at TJ Robert states. "You must be new in
town."

Laughing at this comment TJ replied. "It must be stamped on
my forehead or something, as everyone I talk to says the same
thing."

Looking at the article in TJ's hand, Robert asks if he likes
basketball stories.

BLURRED LINE

"Ya some of them are pretty good."

Hearing a commotion coming towards them, Robert peers around the end of the isle and mutters. "Crap it's Finkelstein." looking back at TJ, Robert warns him. "If I were you I wouldn't wait around for that troublesome newshound. Well it's been a pleasure look me up if you get the chance." then he scurries down another isle to evade detection by Finkelstein.

TJ is highly amused by Robert's antics, and is still grinning when he's approached by an older man who is struggling to regain his breath from running.

Unable to resist TJ sticks out his hand and proclaims. "Hi I'm JT, you must be new in town as I've never seen you before."

Staring at JT in puzzlement he automatically shakes JT's proffered hand and absently replies. "John Finkelstein." as comprehension dawns on him regarding JT's words he smiles and replied "Touché."

Having regained his wind, he asks JT. "Did Robert call me a hack and advise you to run from me?"

"Not really, he just said you like to ask a lot of questions."

Snorting in derision John declares. "Pretty hard to publish a newspaper and not ask questions. So, what brings you to South - Bend?"

"I'm here to visit my Uncle Jebidiah."

"Your Jebidia's nephew?" asked an incredulous Finkelstein staring at TJ.

Now, TJ is thinking he should have left with Robert to avoid the inquisitive reporter.

"I never knew Jeb had family other than his wife Patricia who passed away some time ago." mused Finkelstein. Thinking there would be no harm, TJ informs Finkelstein that Uncle Jebidiah is his father's half-brother.

"What's your father's name?"

"Clive Jackson."

"Interesting, I've never heard of him. Did you know that your Uncle was special forces?"

BLURRED LINE

"Ya I heard something about that, not sure what it means though," answered TJ

"Means you don't fuck with him," Finkelstein stated bluntly. Tiring now of this nosy guy and his questions, TJ, like Robert before him beats a hasty retreat, not allowing Finkelstein the opportunity to ask more questions.

Emerging from the Mercantile, TJ blinks his eyes to adjust to the now bright sunlight. Watching a car roll slowly up to the curb and stop, TJ watches the massive from of Larry unfold from the vehicle and ask. "Hey kid you ready to go?"

Smiling at this offered escape route from the nosy Finkelstein, TJ quickly informs Larry he is more than ready.

"Just throw that ugly suitcase of yours in the back."

Following Larry's instructions, TJ then hops in the front seat. He is amused to see Finkelstein emerge from the store and stare in consternation as he believes another potential Pulitzer prize winning story may have slipped through his fingers.

The ride to Jebs place was a quiet one, TJ is awestruck that there can be this much empty land, being so accustomed to the congestion of the city. TJ does become somewhat concerned when Larry begins to ask questions about where he's from. TJ deliberately keeps his answers vague, hoping to discourage the questions.

"Never been in Metro-City?" questioned Larry.

"Don't think so, my parents didn't like to travel."

"You sort of look familiar, but I must be mistaken."

In an attempt at diverting any further questions, TJ asks Larry how much longer they have till they arrive.

"We're getting close; we've been on his property for about ten minutes now."

"Really!" exclaimed an incredulous TJ.

"Yes, old Jeb has a fair-sized place," commented Larry as they continue to bounce along the rough dusty road.

Emerging from a bend in the road TJ spots a smaller, somewhat dilapidated house perched on a small rise, with a thin

BLURRED LINE

tendril of smoke emitting from the chimney. As they get closer TJ also sees what looks like a swing set made from small logs on the covered veranda. When TJ and Larry exit the vehicle the dust from their arrival lingers in the air, causing TJ to cough briefly. Looking around they hear a door slam, and watch as a tall lanky figure descends from the porch. Quietly watching as the figure approaches, TJ takes in the long unkempt gray hair, with an equally long and unkempt beard. The face is the color of mahogany from years of exposure to sun and wind. He also wonders if his brothers knew their uncle happened to be white.

Stopping ten feet away and studying Larry, Jeb finally speaks in voice laden with disdain. "So, it is you Donovan. I was hoping they were lying when they said you were back."

"Come on Jeb be nice now, I brought your favorite nephew out from town."

"I sure as hell don't recall asking you to do any such thing, and he's not my favorite nephew as I've never met him," declared an irate Jeb. Having said this, Jeb then turns his attention to TJ and studies him up and down. Once again returning his attention back to Larry demands wrathfully. "Why are you still standing here Donovan, get the fuck off my property right now, and next time wait till you're invited!"

TJ was amazed at his uncle's next action, as Jeb spits a seemingly endless stream of foul, brown colored tobacco juice that narrowly missed Larry's shiny boots.

Not deigning to even look where the tobacco juice landed, Larry simply stared at Jeb, then reminded TJ to get his suitcase out of the car.

"I never liked him as a kid, and I sure as hell don't like him as an adult. Now what did you say your name was?"

"I'm calling myself JT. My brothers said I should change my name. My real name is Tyrone Jackson, or TJ."

With a snort of derision Jeb mutters. "Well that's fuckin original. Anyways come on we might as well get you into the house and settled in."

BLURRED LINE

Entering the house TJ is immediately aware of a sound like someone sawing wood. Asking his uncle what that noise is he's told that it is just the old dog snoring. Glancing around the dimly lit interior TJ spots a piano in the far corner. Everything else in the house bears a fine coating of dust, the piano on the other hand gleams as though just recently polished. Watching TJ make his way over to it Jeb asks him if he plays.
"Yes, I really enjoy playing," replied TJ enthusiastically.

"Well that's good to hear, but you won't play that one. That piano was my wife's, no one has played a note on it since she passed away, and no one ever will," warned Jeb. Pointing in the general direction of a closed-door Jeb tells TJ that will be his room and he can put his suitcase in there.

Throwing his suitcase on the bed TJ is not at all surprised to see a small cloud of dust erupt around the edges of the suitcase. TJ cannot believe what his brothers have done, sending me way out here to live with this nutcase. Hearing his name called TJ heads in the direction the voice came from.

"Come in and sit down," ordered his cantankerous uncle who's staring out the small kitchen window. As TJ, does as requested, Jeb asks him if he would like a drink of water. Turning to face the seated TJ he begins speaking. "We have never met before so you can call me Uncle Jeb, or old guy it really makes no difference to me." Studying TJ closer he remarks. "You favor your dad," changing tack he begins again. "Your brothers told me you had girl trouble and you needed to get out of town. With a twinkle in his eye, Jeb tells TJ that he doesn't believe that for a minute as he's way too ugly for any girl to like. "Now if you want you can tell me the real reason you're here that's fine, just don't take me for a fool."

Thinking that the least he can do is be honest, TJ informs his Uncle of the events leading up to his arrival here.

"Well that sure enough isn't girl trouble is it," pondered Jeb as he absorbed all the details. "We have a problem!" declared Jeb. "Up until six months ago, Donovan was a cop in the City."

BLURRED LINE

A surprised Jeb listens, as TJ informs him that he recognized
Larry as one of the cops that used to come to the restaurant
where he is employed as a waiter.

"He never recognized you?"

"No I don't think so as it's been a couple of years since he last
seen me."

"Well if your brothers had told me that, I would have told them
that this might not be safest place for you. Not much we can do
about that now, C'mon I might as well show you around
outside."

Touring the property TJ is amazed at the assortment of animals
his uncle owns, having been raised in the city TJ has never had
the opportunity to see cows and horses.

Pointing to a colorful red rooster he calls Charlie, Jeb warns TJ
to never turn his back to him as he will spur you every time.

"What are spurs?" asked a puzzled TJ.

Pretending to be looking at something else, Jeb slowly
advances towards the chicken. Then with lightning speed catches
the unsuspecting rooster. Walking back to TJ with the rooster
squawking loudly in protest, he points to the wicked looking
appendages protruding from each leg. "Those are spurs, and they
fuckin hurt when he gets you with them," counseled Jeb.

It has been a week now since TJ arrived at his uncle's. The
painful blisters on his hands, are proof that it is anything but an
idyllic interlude for him. He is fast settling into a routine of
mending fences, mucking out barns and dodging the rooster.
Mercifully each night TJ is so exhausted he immediately falls to
sleep with no nightmares featuring the Delveccio brothers. One
night following a delicious supper of burnt stew, TJ asks his
uncle if he would like chicken tomorrow night.

Smiling at TJ, Jeb asks. "Charlie?"

"Ya son of a bitch has got me twice," complained TJ ruefully
rubbing a sore calf.

Chuckling, as he rises from the table Jeb deposits his dishes in
the sink at the same time reminding TJ it's his night for dishes.

BLURRED LINE

"Seems like it's my night every night," groused TJ. "You never heard of an automatic dishwasher?"

"Yes, and I call it TJ", emitting a loud guffaw Jeb makes his way towards the porch for his after-dinner cigar. He is interrupted on his way by the shrilling of the telephone, Jeb looks at his watch and sees its seven pm. "Who the hell is calling at this time of day?" he grumbled out loud. Watching his acerbic uncle, TJ realizes that he is enjoying this time spent with him.

TJ's train of thought is interrupted when his uncle holds the phone out for him and cryptically tells him the caller wants to speak to him.

Surprised, TJ grabs the phone and with excitement evident in his voice barks out. "Mark?"

"No, it's not Mark!" says TJ's mom.

TJ's eyes begin to well up with tears, as it seems an eternity since he has heard his mom's voice.

Feeling that TJ would appreciate some privacy, Jeb once again headed outside to the porch for his after-supper cigar.

"Well Tyrone I'm not very happy with your brothers, Mark has explained everything to me but I still don't understand why you couldn't just go to the police. David insists that the police are not to be trusted, so I must trust your brothers. Mark and I are going to see David next week to resolve this, so that you will be able to come home. Ben called and said you told him that you were going to help an uncle and wonders if you will be home in time for the prom. I love you and miss you terribly son, now put that no good uncle of yours on the phone for me please." Barely able to refrain from sobbing as he says goodbye, he calls for Jeb to come to the phone.

As Jeb re-enters the house, TJ ducks his head to prevent Jeb seeing his tears. Taking a seat on the veranda swing TJ can hear only one side of the conversation his uncle is having with his mom.

"Yes Ophelia. Yes, Ophelia. Will do Ophelia. I understand completely Ophelia. Goodbye Ophelia."

BLURRED LINE

Trailing aromatic cigar smoke, Jeb returned to the veranda and settles down beside TJ on the swing.

"Looks like I will be in hotter water then you're already in if something happens to you on my watch," Jeb stated with a wry grin, while gently nudging the ash from the end of his cigar.

As they both sit there on the swing in companionable silence TJ asks his uncle. "Can you tell me about my dad?"

Studying the glowing end of his cigar Jeb takes his time before answering. "What would you like to know?"

"I don't know, everything I guess. I really miss him. He couldn't even say goodbye," TJ concluded with a hint of residual anger mixed with yearning.

Rotating the end of his cigar on his knee to dislodge the growing length of ash, Jeb begins. "Your dad and I first met when your grandfather married my mom. At that time people were not as accepting of mixed race marriages. They were in love, and their courage surpassed their fears. You might have noticed that I'm white."

"You're kidding, I never noticed." responded TJ dryly.

"Anyways," continued Jeb. "Your dad and I became best friends right away, just as well, as no one else wanted anything to do with us. We learned to depend on each other, our parents were ostracized by both sides of the family. My mom had lifelong friends that turned away from her but, she never regretted for a minute marrying your grandfather."

"So why didn't we even know about you?" asked TJ.

"You did sort of." countered Jeb. "I came to see you and your brothers when you were born. One time your mom and dad brought you guys out here for a visit. I was involved with some pretty bad people in my career, and it was best that they not know about you guys."

"What did you do?"

"Sorry son, can't talk about that". Jeb replied abruptly.

BLURRED LINE

Returning to TJ's original question Jeb continued.
"I have been talking to your dad. Do not think for a minute that he doesn't love and miss you boys." declared Jeb. "Unfortunately your father got caught up in something a lot bigger than him. By the time, he realized he was in trouble it was already too late. He has some demons that need to be tamed, and believe me he is doing his best."

"Yes, well he could have told us himself, instead of just fuckin leaving," proclaimed TJ once again re-living the anger at being abandoned.

"TJ!" barked an irate Jeb. "You might have every right to be angry, but don't talk about your father like that to me. You are young, we humans all make mistakes. If you go through your life and not make any, then and only then you may still want to condemn your father."

Staring at his uncle TJ mutters. "Going to bed." and takes his leave.

Continuing to sit in the now quiet darkness, Jeb shook his head in consternation at his brother's defection, Jeb would gladly re-write his own history for the opportunity to raise TJ and his brothers.

BLURRED LINE

PART THREE

CHAPTER TWENTY-ONE

Entering the South- Bend Police Station, Chief Larry Donovan is always amazed at how spacious it is, relative to the size of the town. Glancing over at his two constables as he seats himself at his desk, a fleeting look of contempt flashes across his countenance.

"Hey Willy, what the fuck you reading now?" demanded Larry.

Holding up the current magazine issue detailing all the latest safety equipment for police officers Willy responds. "Just reading this boss."

"Okay now that I have your undivided attention, I have to return to Metro-City for a couple of days." glancing at Irene with a malicious glare knowing full well that she does not like him continued. "Willy, you will be in charge while I'm gone!" Now openly smiling at Irene upon saying this added. "Not that anything ever happens here."

Opening the locked drawer on his desk, Larry removes some papers, then rising from his desk mutters. "See you in a couple of days."

The door has no sooner closed when Willy apologizes to Irene telling her that it should be her, not him in charge.

"Oh Willy, It's alright. You're now my boss, don't apologize."

After the long drive, back to the City, Larry's mood is not improved when he thinks about the reason for his return. Parking his car in an inconspicuous corner of a large deserted warehouse; Larry walks toward the staircase that leads to the meeting room where his idiot associates better be waiting.

Entering the room and slamming the door closed behind him Larry allows the full fury he is feeling to enter his voice.

BLURRED LINE

"What the fuck are you idiots doing? I leave town for two months and you have everything fucked up. Why did you kill that guy? He owed ten thousand bucks to Tony, now Tony wants me to pay him the fuckin money. How the fuck did you get kill him, from maybe break a leg or arm?"

Knowing they had messed up, and expecting to catch hell for it, Charlie and Vinnie were stunned at the depth of Larry's fury.

As if performing a magic feat, a gun suddenly appears in Larry's massive right hand. "Here's what we're going to do!" Slowly waving the gun at Charlie and Vinnie like the dancing head of a King Cobra, Larry tells them to very carefully place their guns on the table.

With two guns now resting on the table, Larry turns his gun towards Vinnie, and informs him that he has exactly two seconds to put his other gun on the table before he is shot. Grimacing Vinnie relinquishes his second weapon.

"Now that's better boys." Spinning a chair around, then sitting on the backwards facing chair, Larry begins to speak. "Charlie, you have exactly one hour to bring me ten thousand bucks." Holding up his gun as if to ward off any objections continues. "I will be holding brother Vinnie here as collateral." looking at his watch then up at Charlie, asks him. "Why are you still here? You have just wasted three minutes."

Realizing that Larry is deadly serious Charlie quickly rises from his chair and with a muttered curse heads out the door. In the exactly forty-three minutes it took Charlie to return with the money, not a single word was exchanged between Larry and Vinnie.

"See that wasn't too difficult was it," stated Larry in a voice laden with sarcasm.

Pointing to the valise containing the ten thousand dollars, Larry announced. "Now that you have generously donated this money, where are we at with this kid that seen you two idiots?"

"We went to the cops and Vinnie here filed a report of assault and battery, the cops have the basketball that was used.

BLURRED LINE

Some kid found it and took it home, his parents thought it was covered in dried blood, so being law abiding citizens took it to the cops. A source of mine with the cops, has told me that they showed the ball to some kids and one kid thought it was his friends ball. This kid said his friends name is Tyrone Jackson, but the kid said that TJ has gone to his uncles," concluded Charlie.

Digesting what he has been told by Charlie, Larry sums it up. "So, we have the cops trying to locate this Tyrone Jackson, who witnessed you guys kill that guy. What do we know about this Jackson kid? Is he White, Black, big, small?"

Feeling relieved they're still breathing, Charlie continues. "I knew a Clive Jackson; he was heavy into the needle. He once said he had a half-brother somewhere but I can't remember where, I bet the kid is hiding out there."

Staring at the brothers, Larry calmly informs them. "My initial reaction was to come here tonight, just shoot the both of you then burn the building down around you. What I will do is take this money to Tony, I will be staying at the Travelers Motel on First street, you better have a name for me before I leave town tomorrow night!"

Angry, and resenting the way Larry has treated them, Vinnie breaks his silence. "Hey Larry, don't forget we know about all the shit you've done. You treat us like morons yet we're the ones doing all your dirty work. Whenever you have a problem that needs to be cleaned up you call us. So maybe think about getting off that fucking high horse you're on and treat us with some respect."

Staring at Vinnie for thirty seconds, Larry tells him with a voice carved from ice. "If that was supposed to be a threat Vinnie, then consider yourself already dead." Pointing at the guns on the table Larry suggests. "If either one, or even both of you feel lucky, then by all means go for your guns.

BLURRED LINE

When I leave, you two sit here and hold each other's hands for twenty minutes, or whatever you want to do, but leave here before twenty and all bets are off," with that said Larry unloads all three weapons residing on the table, and opening the door to the room tosses the bullets to the floor below.

CHAPTER TWENTY-TWO

It's 10 am at the state penitentiary, David is quietly reading in his jail cell waiting for the guard to escort him to the library to continue his studies. He looks up as he hears the heavy tread of approaching footsteps.

"Jackson, you have a visitor," announced the guard.

This news surprises David, as he was not expecting his mom and brother Mark until tomorrow. Towering over the guard at six feet seven inches, David falls in behind the guard for the long walk to the visitor's area. As the guard fails to make the turn into the visitor's room, David smiles and remarks. "I think we missed our turn."

With a humorless grunt the guard responds. "Supposed to take you to the private rooms."

Not having any meeting planned with his lawyer, David's curiosity is piqued as they head to the private meeting rooms, upon entering the room, David sees someone vaguely familiar seated at the table.

Standing up Detective Mike Chance, reaches out to shake David's hand, and seeing the puzzled look on his face reminds him who he is, and that he used to play basketball against David some years ago.

Feeling his phone vibrate with an incoming call, Mike impatiently removes it from his pocket, and is about to turn it off when he sees his old Lieutenant's name on caller display. Mike listens to what Jim has to say, then looking completely dumbfounded thanks him and ends the call.

BLURRED LINE

Again, apologizing to David for the interruption, informs him he must make a call. Calling the precinct house Mike asks to speak to Sergeant O'Mallory, he is told that the sergeant has left the precinct.

With a thoughtful look on his face, Mike picks up where he left off. "It's really good seeing you again David. Quite a coincidence having played basketball against both you and your brother Tyrone.

Seeing the surprise on David's face when he mentioned Tyrone, Mike explains. "I first met Tyrone when I ate at Miguel's. Unfortunately, it appears that Tyrone may have witnessed an event that could place him in harm's way. I have been trying to locate your brother to ensure his wellbeing but, even your mom has resisted in telling me his whereabouts. I'm afraid that the cop who questioned some kids about a basketball might be connected to the perpetrators of the alleged killing. Some kid named Ben Harris advised the cop that Tyrone had said he was going to his uncle's place. Now these guys aren't stupid, they know that Clive Jackson is your father. These are the very people that supplied your father with drugs, so I don't think it will take them long to figure out who the uncle is."

Listening with rapt attention, David has not allowed his face to give anything away. Wrestling with a natural inclination to not believe a cop, David comes to grips with the fact that this cop might be the only one to save his brother's life. Therefore, he somewhat reluctantly reveals to Mike, that his brother Tyrone is at their Uncle Jebidiah's place in South -Bend.

"That's interesting David, my old partner is now the Chief of Police in South bend."

Once again feeling the telltale vibration of an incoming call, Mike looks at David, and shrugging his shoulders in resignation takes the call.

Pushing his chair back from the table in a lame attempt at giving Mike some privacy, David crosses his arms on his chest and feigns interest in the tile pattern on the floor.

BLURRED LINE

It is only when he hears Mike ended the call, that he looks up and is shocked at how red Mike's face is.

"We have a major fucking problem David, for obvious reasons I can only divulge certain parts of that conversation to you. It seems that my ex-partner Larry is alleged to have close ties to the very people that Tyrone is hiding from. This puts your brother in grave danger if Larry discovers he is the one who witnessed the murder.

As David assimilates this information he moans out loud. "For fucks sake, I thought I was helping TJ by sending him to Jebs. Now I might be responsible for getting him killed!"

"Hold on David," remonstrated Mike. "As far as I know, Larry is not aware that it's your brother he is looking for. What's your uncle's phone number? We need to get in touch with him and warn him." Punching the numbers that David recites, Mike hears the phone ringing, after six rings he looks over at David and asks. "No answering machine?"

"Shit, I was surprised he even had a phone, so I doubt he has a machine."

Mike rises from his chair and moves to the locked door of the meeting room, where upon he knocks on the door to gain the guards attention. When the guard pokes his head in, Mike instructs him to bring a phone in for David to use. Once the phone is in place he urges David to keep trying his uncle. Mike advises David that he must leave to attend to other urgent business, but he has every intention of getting to South -Bend as soon as humanly possible to confront Larry. Giving David his cell number, he tells him he wants to know if David talks to Jeb. Looking at the expression on David's face, Mike can only hope they can safely extricate Tyrone from this grave situation.

Leaving the grounds of the penitentiary, Mike activates his lights and siren to expedite his trip back to the precinct. He is still in shock over the phone call from his old boss Jim Nicholas who remembered that Ellen,

BLURRED LINE

his daughter's care giver is Sergeant O'Mallory's niece. He is baffled that O'Mallory did not mention that.

Arriving at the precinct Mike hustles to the booking cells where he has been told that Curly, a low-level drug trafficker is being held. As he makes his way through the hallway, and into the holding cell area, Mike is greeted by the arresting officers.

"Hey Mike." Nodding their heads in the direction of a very disconsolate Curly sitting on the bunk in the cell, they advised Mike that he claims to have vitally important information for him.

"Was someone coming down from the D. A's office?" queried Mike.

"Ya" replied one of the arresting officers. "Al Coltrane said he would be here shortly."

"Not very often you get the big guy himself, he must think this will be good for his career," mused a cynical Mike.

Turning to the cells to face Curly, Mike smiled when he notices that Curly's jaw is somewhat askew.

"Nice jaw you got there Curly." Mike clearly remembers the day that his ex- partner Larry punched Curly.

"Ya fuck you Mike!"

Hearing the door to the holding cell area open, Mike and the two street cops greet Al Coltrane. Someone years ago, dubbed him "Big Al Coltrane" but lacking his custom designed shoes he stands a mere five feet four inches. It's when he's in a courtroom that he becomes a giant to contend with.

Acknowledging the two street cops with a wave of his hand, Al turns to Mike and not mincing any words states sarcastically. "Let's hear what this person of sterling character has to say."

Gazing at the wasted figure with the crooked jaw, Mike orders Curly to tell them what he knows.

"I want a deal before I say a word," squawked a defiant Curly.

"Hey you wanted to fuckin talk, then talk, we don't have all day to waste," commanded an impatient Mike.

BLURRED LINE

Seeing that Curly is being obstinate, Mike decides to call his bluff and says to Al. "C'mon let's go, this son of bitch is jerking our chain."

"Okay, Okay," a desperate Curly capitulates. Glaring at Mike he bleats. "Your partner Donovan is one bad ass son of a bitch. He ordered the Delveccio's to kill his wife in a fake hit and run!"

This immediately re-captured Mike and Al's waning interest in the low-level drug trafficker.

"What did you say?" demanded Al.

"Word is his wife found out about what he does, and was going to call Mike of all people. Guess she never got the chance seeing as how she's dead."

"What proof do you have?" growled Mike

"Charlie and Vinnie told me all about it. Then they took the car to Alfred's to get crushed, from what the brothers told me, you almost got there in time."

As Mike mulled this information over he was almost physically sick to his stomach, as he once again visualizes Maria's terrifying final moments.

With the contempt that he feels for Curly clearly evident in his scathing tone of voice, Mike growled. "So, even though you knew about the hit and run, you did nothing about it until you thought it might be to your advantage in brokering some sort of deal with the District Attorney's office. You are without a doubt Curly, a fuckin gutless wonder, and the poorest excuse of a human being."

Shrugging his thin shoulders, Curly appears not to be bothered at all by Mike's summation.

"What I should do Curly, is take you out to Jo's, march you inside and in a loud voice thank you for all your help. I sincerely doubt you would survive twenty-four hours."

"You can't do that," whined the pitiful creature. "I made a deal with him," pointing at Al

BLURRED LINE

"I'm not sure what kind of fuckin deal you think you have Curly," looking over his shoulder at the other two cops Mike asks them if they heard anything about a deal. They both deny hearing any such thing. By this time Curly is on the verge of tears.

Al then asks Curly. "What do you know about this latest killing?"

"The brothers were really scared, they were only supposed to lean on this Harris guy, but they got carried away. They told me that Larry just might kill both of them. Then when they realized there was a witness they were really scared."

"So how is it that Larry knows these Delveccio brothers?"

"Holy shit, you don't know do you?" exclaimed Curly.

Once again Mike allows the impatience he's feeling to enter his voice. "For fuck sake's Curly do I have to drag every goddamn word out of you?"

Knowing that Mike could very well make good on his threat, the words began pouring from Curly's mouth. "They grew up together in some hick town called South -Bend, from what they have told me Larry hated his old man. The Delveccio's would beat the shit out of Larry, who then went to the cops and tried to have his old man arrested, but the cops weren't buying it. So, one night when Larry was about sixteen Charlie, Vinnie, and Larry beat him to death. Vinnie said they took the body to some river, weighed it down with an anvil and tossed him in," pausing to catch his breath Curly once again begins his narrative. "With Larry's old man reported missing the cops started looking pretty hard at the three boys. Charlie, Vinnie, and their younger sister Ellen, left their alcoholic parents and came here to the City to live with their Uncle, Gwyn O'Mallory."

At this juncture, all three cops are staring at Curly.

Mike was shocked to learn that his daughter's caregiver, was a sibling to two of the worst criminals in the city.

BLURRED LINE

Absorbing this new information, Al realized that this is how the Delveccio's have eluded serious jail time.

Mike is completely flabbergasted at this point, Larry grew up with the Delveccio's, whose uncle just happens to be the guy that hates Mike.

Having for the most part maintained a steely silence throughout Curly's revelations, Al abruptly informs Mike he has heard enough. He will have arrest warrants issued for the Delveccio brothers, Larry, as well as O'Mallory.

They should be on Mike's desk within the hour, then in complete disgust comments. "No wonder the public has nothing but contempt for this fucking PD. If we can't police ourselves how can we expect the public to trust us?"

Running his hand through his unruly, curly black hair, Mike attempts to formulate some sort of plan to deal with the ramifications arising from Curly's information. Heading upstairs to the sanctuary of his own desk, he takes a short detour to see the desk sergeant, arriving at the desk Mike asks the duty sergeant as to O'Mallory's whereabouts.

"Dunno, he just put in for his annual leave time and left."

Feeling stymied at being unable to question O'Mallory about his niece, Mike resumes his way to his own desk upstairs. Seated at his desk Mike is completely baffled by O'Mallory's silence about his relationship to Ellen. He also remembers the geriatric neighbor mentioning that the day after his girls went missing, someone picked up Ellen. *"Was that someone O'Mallory"*. He asks himself.

Taking Larry's whole fabrication concerning his father, and abusing the public's trust in the PD as a personal affront, Mike now considers Larry to be the worst kind of criminal. Jotting some notes on his legal pad allows Mike to better see, and prioritize a plan of action. Locating the phone number for the South- Bend Police Department and places a call to them.

BLURRED LINE

When the call is answered, Mike identifies himself and asks who he is speaking with.

"This is constable Irene Ingalls's."

"Hello Irene, I don't expect you to believe me so please call the Metro-city PD and ask to speak to Detective Mike Chance. They will direct your call to my cell phone."

Hardly a minute goes by when Mike feels his cell phone vibrate, answering it he is greeted by Irene.

"Okay Irene, whereabouts is Larry Donovan right now?"

"He left yesterday for Metro-City, said he would be gone for a couple of days."

"Holy shit!" exclaimed Mike. "He's here in the city?"

"That's where he said he was going; I have no means to verify his actual whereabouts."

Mike is ecstatic with this news if he can only somehow locate and arrest Larry while he is here in town then TJ will be safe.

Mike hears Irene saying "Hello? Hello?"

"Sorry about that Irene, I was busy thinking. Would it be possible for you to go to Jebidiah Walker's place, locate Tyrone Jackson and place him in protective custody? Actually, I believe he may be using an alias."

Not understanding who this Tyrone Jackson is and his connection to Jebidiah, she asks Mike for clarification.

Mike relates to Irene a condensed version of what has taken place and why TJ is at Jebs.

"Holy shit, are you kidding me?" breathed Irene

"I wish I was," replied Mike

"That son of a bitch Larry, comes here and takes what should have been my position, and he's nothing but a low life criminal."

"It would appear that's the case. "So, about TJ?" prompted Mike.

"Oh right." Irene then gives Mike her cell phone number, advising him that cell service there is sketchy at the best of times.

BLURRED LINE

Knowing now that TJ is not in any immediate danger, and that in a short time he should be in protective custody. Mike places a call to the State Penitentiary and has their office deliver a message to David informing him of this.

Consulting his hastily scribbled notes, Mike bends his head down and rests it on joined fingers. The remorse he is feeling for Maria is almost overwhelming, she never stood a chance against Larry's inherent malice. He can now only think of his ex-partner with loathing, contempt, and sincerely hopes that Larry will resist arrest.

Hearing someone clear their throat in an unobtrusive manner to get his attention, Mike looks up to see a message runner bearing the promised arrest warrants.

Having the arrest warrants in his hand Mike faces a dilemma, attempt to serve the warrants on persons whose whereabouts are unknown, or drive to South -Bend and ensure TJ's safety. Realizing full well he has no legal jurisdiction there, he never the less decides saving that kids life, is his priority.

After advising his Lieutenant of his plans to drive to South - Bend in the morning, he places a call to Irene's cell phone and as expected could not reach her.

CHAPTER TWENTY-THREE

"Hey Larry it's Charlie."

"No fuckin kidding," Larry barks in a voice filled with contempt. "Hey you want to meet Vinnie and me at the same warehouse tomorrow morning at seven am. We're gonna go lean on a guy and get that kids uncles name for you."

"Okay," agreed Larry.

Surprised at how easy that was Charlie stammers out. "Uh okay then."

Hanging up the phone Larry laughed mirthlessly. How stupid do they think he is?

The following morning Larry parks his car two blocks away from the predetermined meeting place at five am. Quickly walking to the warehouse in the cool predawn darkness, Larry ascends the staircase and makes himself comfortable. Not in the least bit surprised he hears the noise of the Delveccio's arriving at six am.

As the brothers enter the already lit room, Charlie asks no one. "Why the fuck are the lights already on?" The surprise at seeing Larry already seated in the room is clearly etched on Charlie's face.

With his weapon trained on the brothers, Larry drawls. "Good morning boys, glad you could make it. A tad early but no problem. Okay you know the drill, weapons on the table."

Shocked at seeing Larry already seated in the room, the brothers dismally realize their attempt at subterfuge has failed miserably. Following Larry's directions albeit reluctantly, they toss their weapons on the table.

BLURRED LINE

"Now grab a chair and push it against that far wall and make yourselves comfortable."

Abandoning his chair for the more advantageous position directly across from them, Larry notices the brothers quickly glance at each other. Clearly able to interpret their thought process Larry barks out a guffaw. "That's right guys there are two of you and one of me. Now I'm not invincible and one of you just might get lucky and get me, but which one of you is prepared to die?" casually waving his gun at each of them he continued. "One or both of you will die, that's a guarantee. So, we can either see who's toughest, or we can sit here like gentlemen and discuss this situation," he finished with a smile that never came close to reaching his eyes.

At this juncture, Vinnie decides to speaks up. "Ya Larry we found that guy and he gave up the uncle's name. It's some guy named Jebidiah Walker, and he lives in of all places fuckin South -Bend."

As Larry digests this information, he realizes that he had the fuckin kid in his car, and that he delivered the kid to his uncle. "Jesus Christ," he mutters in exasperation. Motioning for the brothers to sit Larry rises from his chair and leans against the wall.

Knowing full well that the brothers had every intention of arriving early this morning to set a trap for him, Larry ponders his next move.

Sensing that their lives may be hanging in the balance, Charlie attempts to appease Larry with some unrelated information. "You know Mike, that old partner of yours."

Snapped out of his thought process by this statement Larry snarls at Charlie. "Of course, I know him you moron."

Finding Larry's response inoffensive Charlie resumes. "Uncle Gwyn hated that guy, he said that Mike needed to be taken down a notch. Uncle Gwyn overheard Mike one day saying they needed a caregiver for their girls. He had Ellen call the wife and being desperate she hired Ellen."

BLURRED LINE

Getting impatient, Larry barks at Charlie. "What's your fuckin point?"

Once again ignoring Larry's outburst Charlie points at Vinnie and continues. "One day Vinnie here was on a computer, and seen an ad by a couple wanting to adopt two kids. We arranged a meeting with them and they made it clear that they were willing to pay big bucks for some kids. They didn't want to wait for them, they wanted them now!"

Starting to realize where this is going Larry barked. "How much?"

"Twenty grand," piped up a beaming Vinnie

"Total?" asked Larry.

Still beaming Vinnie replies. "Hell no, twenty grand per kid."

Jumping back into the conversation Charlie picks up where he left off. "So, we were wondering where the fuck we could get two girls from."

That's when Uncle Gwyn suggested we grab Mikes kids, it was like takin candy from a kid. Ellen didn't want any part of it, until we told her we would give her five grand to get the hell out of town."

Charlie and Vinnie are now beginning to think they should have kept their mouths shut, as they witness Larry's countenance darken like a fast-approaching storm.

With his eyes throwing daggers at the brothers, a thoroughly enraged Larry bellowed. "Where in the fuck is my share?"

In the face of Larry's wrath Charlie sullenly replied. "Gwyn told us that since you weren't in on it then you don't get a cut."

"Oh, he did, did he. Well he's fuckin wrong as usual. Where are those people that bought the girls?"

"Vinnie did some investigating and found out where they live."

"Write down their name and address for me." demanded Larry

"What are you going to do Larry? They live three thousand miles away," asked a tremulous Vinnie.

BLURRED LINE

"Well apparently, they didn't know about me I will pay them a visit and explain to them the power of the media.
I'm sure they will choose the right course of action and I will leave with a pocket full of cash." In a calmer, but far more deadly tone of voice Larry explained to the brothers they need to tell him truthfully why they showed up an hour before the scheduled meet time.

Looking helplessly at each other, Charlie shrugs his shoulders in resignation and decides to answer. "We were going to try to kill you," he stated unequivocally.

Larry steps over to the table and moves the weapons farther away from the brothers, winking at them he comments. "Just in case you try something stupid."

With these words, Vinnie and Charlie seriously begin to question whether they will leave this place alive.

Seeming to enjoy their discomfort Larry is in no hurry to divulge his plans for them. Then deciding that they have sweated enough he begins to speak. "It appears we have a reached a cross road in our relationship, I can no longer trust you. I knew what you were planning for me this morning, that's why I arrived an hour before you guys. We have a choice to make, either I kill you both right now and leave," adding "You likely won't be found before the maggots have had a feast." "The other option is we all leave here together and never see, or contact each other again."
"I kind of like the second option Larry," murmured a hopeful Charlie.

Vinnie nodded his head in agreement.

"Funny, I thought you guys might like that one better, leave your guns where they are, and you gentlemen can walk down the stairs in front of me."

Larry followed the brothers as they exit the room, and with practiced ease quickly threads a silencer on to his weapon.

BLURRED LINE

The Delveccios wear minuscule smiles of relief on their faces
as they begin to descend the stairs, Charlie is already planning to
kill Larry at the first opportunity.

That's as far as the thought went, with two barely audible burps
issuing from Larry's weapon, both brothers were dead before
their tumbling bodies reached the bottom of the stairs in a
tangled mass of human detritus. Stepping gingerly over the
lifeless forms of the brothers, Larry wearing a rueful smile
realizes he forgot to ask them where the money is.

Even though Larry has known the brothers for many years,
there was no way in hell he could trust them any longer. He
knows that the brothers would have sold him out to the cops with
no hesitation if they were ever caught.

He has no illusions about how much time he will have to serve
if he is ever arrested, and a cop in a penitentiary usually doesn't
last long. With a last look at the brothers, Larry turns and leaves
the warehouse. Whistling tunelessly, he quickly covers the two
blocks to his car, the only living thing he encounters is a curious
raccoon.

Seated in his car he has already forgotten the brothers, and is
charting his next course of action. Glancing at the scrap of paper
that Vinnie had written Alicia and Desiree s names on, he
memorizes the name and address of the buyers. Larry then
absently tosses the scrap of paper on to the car floor. Deciding
that for the present O'Mallory and his niece Ellen posed no
threat, he heads back to South -Bend to deal with that kid.

CHAPTER TWENTY-FOUR

Jeb and TJ are blissfully unaware of the quickly approaching tempest, they are on their third and final day of an impromptu fishing trip. Jeb had decided that TJ needed a break from the drudgery of farm chores. Saddling up his two horses along with his pack mule, Jeb took TJ to a magical place. After six long hours in the saddle they left the cactus strewn ridge, and descend into what appears to be a miniature canyon. The arid, dust filled previous six hours is now replaced by lush grasses, the air they breathe is redolent with the fragrance of Ponderosa Pine trees. Seeing TJ's rapture mirrored on his face, Jeb informs him the best is yet to come. Riding his horse through the gently waving knee high grass, TJ doubts this can get better. A brief ten minutes later as they round a bend, TJ spies a slowly meandering river with the sunlight shimmering on the surface. Jeb comes to a halt in a small clearing surrounded by stately pine trees, TJ is afraid that if he pinches himself he will wake up from this dream.

The next three days were the best and the worst of TJ's life. Uncle Jeb decided that TJ needed to learn the fine art of Fly Fishing. TJ has never thought fishing could be so frustrating, his fly has caught nearby trees, his hat, but most embarrassing was the fact he caught no fish. Jeb meanwhile seems to catch a glistening Rainbow Trout on every cast, all the while explaining the art of dancing your fly across the water. Throwing his rod in frustration onto the nearby bank, TJ begins disrobing. Watching his nephew's antics and laughing uproariously Jeb manages to ask TJ. "What are you doing son?"

BLURRED LINE

Removing his last stitch of clothing, TJ declares he's going swimming. Diving into the deep, cool, clear water, TJ re-emerges and releases a long, drawn out wail that emanates from his soul, venting the frustration he feels at how much his life has been altered, through no fault of his own.

Rolling over onto his back TJ is completely in the moment, looking up at the scattered wisps of clouds fervently wishing this would last forever.

He is therefore surprised, when from right beside him he hears Jeb ask him. "Better now son?"

"Yes" is TJ's simple answer.

With both Jeb and TJ out of the river, and back into dry clothes Jeb informs TJ that they will break camp and head home.

CHAPTER TWENTY-FIVE

Arriving back in South -Bend, Larry proceeds to his temporary
residence to exchange his personal vehicle with his official
vehicle. Ducking into his house for a quick shower and change
of clothes, he sits down on the lone dilapidated chair at the card
table, to decide how he should address this issue with TJ.

While Larry is sitting at his table, Mike is arriving at the South-
Bend Police Department. Walking through the door he is amazed
at how spacious and orderly the office is, this is so completely
different than the daily chaos back home, if it were not for the
sign on the desk welcoming you to the South -Bend Police
Department, he would have sworn he was in the wrong place.
Seeing a lady typing at one of the three desks, Larry politely
clears his throat to get her attention. As she looks up, Mike
catches a flash of irritation cross her freckled face at this
unexpected intrusion. Mike apologizes for the intrusion, and asks
if Irene Ingalls is available. It is her turn to apologize stating as
she rises from her desk. "I didn't hear you come in."

Mike is rendered speechless, it has been approximately eight
months since his daughters have disappeared, and shortly
thereafter his wife Adele left him. He has until this moment been
an island unto himself, the pain and anguish he has suffered with
his double loss has crippled his ability to relate to others.
Until now. Feeling much like a young man about to ask a girl for
a date, Mike's tongue suddenly feels too large for his mouth.
Feeling himself stare, he watches the incredibly attractive form
of Irene approach the counter.

BLURRED LINE

Absorbing the light brown hair that barely touches her shoulders, the pert nose sprinkled with freckles, eyes the color of bright emeralds. He is lost.

Seeing the way, she has affected this stranger, Irene is torn between feeling offended, or flattered, placing both her hands on the counter she asks. "How may I help?"

Mike is intrigued when he sees no evidence of a ring on any of her fingers, realizing she has asked him a question, Mike introduced himself.

After the introductions, Mike asks her where TJ is.

"I don't know? I went out to Jebs like you requested, there was no one around, I looked around his property and noticed his horses and mule were gone. I was planning on going out there this afternoon to see if they have returned."

"Have you heard from Larry?"

"Not since he left. If he's back, he hasn't notified us."

Thinking about this, Mike suggests they take a drive out to Jebs.

"Sounds good, just let me get Willy." striding down a short hallway she bangs on the men's washroom door and yells. "Hey Willie let's go!"

Seeing the puzzled look on Mikes face, she informs him that Willy is the other full time constable. Winking at Mike she states that Willy enjoys reading his police magazines where he won't be disturbed.

"What did you want Irene?" asked Willy emerging from the washroom.

Performing the introductions, Irene then advises Willy they are going out to Jebs and that he might as well come too.

As they negotiate the last bend in the road and can see Jebs house. Irene murmurs in dismay. "Oh shit!"

Willy pipes up from the back seat. "Hey that looks like Larry's car."

BLURRED LINE

Seeing that the look on Irene's face confirms what Willy has said, Mike unobtrusively slides his weapon out and racks a round into the chamber then engages the safety. Irene notices this action and nods her head in silent affirmation.

As their car comes to halt with the ever-present dust hanging in the air, the three people emerge and closing the car doors begin to walk up the short incline to the house.

With the late afternoon sun behind Jebs house the front porch was bathed in dark shadow, it was only when the big man spoke that they realized Larry was comfortably seated on the porch swing. "Hey Irene, Willy, what brings you guys out here?", an instant later he recognizes Mike. "What the fuck are you doing out here buddy?" Rising from the swing, Larry places a hand on the porch railing and lightly vaults to the yard below, and walks to within ten feet of the waiting trio.

Mike is unable to control his fury at seeing this cold-blooded murderer, in one smooth motion Mike's weapon is in his hand, cocked and ready to fire. Pointing it at Larry, Mike announces that Larry is under arrest for conspiracy to commit murder.

To Mike's utter amazement, Larry begins to laugh. "You have absolutely no jurisdiction here asshole. Who the fuck do you think you are, coming out here to arrest me?" Still chortling as though he has been told a good joke Larry continues. "You poor misguided fool, to think you actually believed you could arrest me," shaking his head in sympathy at Mike's foolishness, Larry does not notice Irene draw her weapon.

"He might not have jurisdiction here Larry, but I sure do and I'm placing you under arrest for suspicion of murder."

At this juncture, Willy lets out a yelp of surprise and asks Irene what she's doing arresting their boss.

"Never mind Willy," is her curt response. Not allowing her attention to waver from Larry for an instant, she then orders Larry to very carefully throw his weapon to the ground.

BLURRED LINE

With two guns pointed at him, Larry realizes that for now he needs to adhere to Irene's orders. Irene then orders Larry to lean against the car, and place his hands behind him. Nodding her head in the direction of the handcuffs located on her belt, Mike grabs them and savoring the moment he quickly and with significantly more force then necessary slaps them on Larry's wrists.

While this is being played out, all Willy can do is stand there in complete stupefaction.

Appearing to be unperturbed that he is now in handcuffs, Larry nonchalantly turns around and leans against the car. Although Larry is in handcuffs, Mike and Irene do not trust the big man enough to re-holster their weapons. They continue to hold them only now they are pointed at the ground.

Directing his comments to Mike, Larry begins speaking in a sarcastic and condescending tone. "So, Mike it's nice to see you too asshole, how you been? Still riding that fuckin white horse, I see. So, you want to arrest me for murder, who is the poor unfortunate soul I murdered?

"Your wife!" growled Mike.

"Well there you go; see I have already solved this horrific event, as you know I was up here considering the Chiefs job."

"Oh, don't worry Larry it's been solved alright." Mike is being very circumspect as he does not want Larry to know their informant is Curly. "The D. A's office heard testimony from an informant, and immediately issued warrants for yourself, the Delveccios as well as O'Mallory."

Chuckling, Larry retorted. "Throw a big enough net Mike you're bound to catch some sucker fish," then with an exaggerated wink he stated. "You may have a problem serving those warrants on the Delveccio's, I hear their pretty close mouthed these days."

"Well Larry, seems like the Delveccios like to talk, they told this person that you grew up with the Delveccios right here in South -Bend, imagine that."

BLURRED LINE

"Like I said Buddy, good luck with those warrants. You know Mike, I almost envy your naivety you think you can save the world. Well news flash buddy, they don't want to be saved. You ever hear someone thank you for arresting them, no they get pissed because they get caught. My advice to you buddy is shoot the fuckin white horse and get a black one with a matching hat," chuckling at his own witty cynicism Larry finally shut up.

Although Irene and Willy were rapt spectators of this conversation, Irene decides that it's time she jumped into this verbal jousting match.

"Okay, enough of this, Willy put the prisoner in the back seat of the Chiefs car and head back to the office. We'll be right behind you."

Feigning a cough to get her attention Larry admonishes Irene. "Hey, I'm still chief, so actually it's my car."

"No, you're not Mr. Donovan," insisted Irene. "You're now my prisoner, and as such you will be driven by Willy to the jail in town and be processed."

Poor Willy at this point is almost beside himself, torn between his friendship with Irene, and worshiping Larry, he turns to Irene to argue.

Knowing what Willy was going to do, Irene held up her hand and manages to curb whatever it is Willy was about to say.

"Mike will give you a hand to get him in the car."

"Fuck that!" barked Larry. "Come on Willy, let's go for a ride." Heading over to the car and while waiting for Willy, he decides that he will sit on the information regarding Mike's girls. He may need that information to extricate himself from his current predicament.

"That's okay boss, you can ride up front with me," murmured a hesitant Willy

"Willy, he is a prisoner, so, he will ride in the back seat!" admonished Irene.

BLURRED LINE

Looking up at Larry, and shrugging his shoulders helplessly Willy assists Larry into the back seat.

Watching as the car pulls away, Mike is already pondering Larry's words regarding the Delveccio's. He fully realizes that Larry will stop at nothing to achieve his goals, hearing a horse nicker, Mike looks up to see Jeb and TJ mounted on their horses emerge from the thinning brush.

"Wasn't exactly expecting a welcome home party," groused Jeb with a questioning look at Irene and Mike.

As Jeb and TJ rein in their horses a few short steps away from Mike and Irene, recognition flashes across TJ's face when he realizes who is with Irene.

"Hello TJ, long time no see," declared Mike with a huge smile at seeing him safe and sound. adding. "You look like you belong on that horse."

Grimacing TJ informs Mike that muscles he didn't know he had, hurt.

Chuckling at this, Mike informs TJ that he's never had the pleasure of riding a horse.

Returning to the reason they are here, Mike tells TJ that it's safe for him to return home, he can ride back to town with him and Irene once he's ready to go.

Quickly dismounting TJ hands his horses reins to Jeb, and hurries off to the house to pack his meager belongings.

Watching TJ with a smile, Jeb turns and with a ferocious look at Mike spoke. "You better be absolutely certain it's safe for that boy. If anything happens to him, I will hold you responsible."

Irene jumps in, and informs Jeb that they have arrested Larry Donovan, adding. "It seems the line between right and wrong has become somewhat blurred to Mr. Donovan."

Grunting at this information. "Never did like that son of a bitch. He's twisted inside," avowed Jeb.

Further conversation is halted when the trio hear the clear, sharp notes of a piano. Thrusting the reins of both horses into a surprised Mike's hand, Jeb hurries off to his house.

BLURRED LINE

Looking quizzically at Irene, she takes the reins from Mike and walks off to a nearby water trough where the grateful horses nosily slake their thirst.

Entering his house, Jeb is not the least bit surprised to see his nephew seated at the piano. Hearing the musical notes rise from the piano, drives home the fact how much he has missed his wife and her music. Walking over to TJ, he places his hand on TJ's shoulder, closes his eyes and allows the music to re-enter his being. At the end of the piece TJ looks up at his uncle and asks. "Better?"

"Yes," is Jeb's one-word reply.

CHAPTER TWENTY-SIX

Larry patiently waited all of five uncomfortable minutes before he began haranguing Willy. With a note of exasperation, he explains to Willy that Mike is jealous of Larry. Ever since their days as patrolman, Mike has envied Larry's ability to catch the bad guys, Larry never expected Mike's jealousy to get this bad. Hearing only the occasional non-committal grunt from Willy, Larry tries a different approach. He attempts to convince Willy that if he were to see Larry's side and end this whole foolish arrest business, Willy would be made acting Chief of Police. Larry would personally see to it that Willy received a car of his own for work. It was these last words that seemed to have the desired effect. Larry begins to feel the car slow down, then the rough bumps of the shoulder before the car comes to a halt. Not wanting to over- sell his strategy Larry remains quiet.
"I will have my own car, and be acting Chief?" queried an excited Willy
"That's correct Willy, and everyone in town will know that you're my right-hand man."
  Appearing to arrive at a decision, Willy slams the transmission lever into park, and gets out of the vehicle. Opening the back door, he watches Larry with his hands manacled behind his back struggle out of the car. Once out of the car, Larry turns his back to Willy so he can release the cuffs. With a sigh of relief Larry rubs his sore wrists, meanwhile Willy has turned back towards the front of the car when Larry barks out his name.

BLURRED LINE

Turning to see what Larry wants, Willy never knew what hit
him. With one punch from the big man, Willy was sprawled on
the ground out cold.

"You stupid sack of shit, you should know not to believe the guy
in cuffs, but in this case, I'm really glad you did." Then as
though adding an exclamation mark Larry kicks Willy as hard as
he can in the ribs.

Removing Willy's handgun, and placing the cuffs on the prone
Willy, Larry casually picks him up and unceremoniously throws
him onto the backseat of the car.

Thinking about where they are, Larry remembers a seldom used
road not far away. Rolling over the rough gravel road has caused
Willy to regain consciousness, struggling to sit up he winces
with pain from his already swollen jaw. "Why did you sucker
punch me?" complained a bewildered Willy.

Ignoring him Larry continues driving until he finds the perfect
spot, stopping the car, he hops out, and opening the rear door
grabs Willy by his hair and drags him out of the vehicle.

"What the fuck Larry? You don't have to kill me!" protested
Willy, who is becoming very aware that his time on earth might
be measured in minutes. Determined to demonstrate his courage
he shakes off Larry's hand and informs him that he can fuckin
walk on his own.

"Head over behind that little hill then asshole," continuing. "You
know Willy I wouldn't have to do this if you had shot Mike and
Irene for me."

"Why the fuck would I shoot Irene and that Mike guy?"
enquired Willy.

"If you have to ask that question Willy, that means I can't count
on you when the chips are down," shaking his head as if in regret
adds. "Therefore, that makes you expendable buddy."

"You're a fuckin loony. You know that Larry. Your fuckin
nuts!" roared a defiant Willy.

"That's far enough Willy, keep facing that way and you won't
see it coming."

BLURRED LINE

Turning to face his executioner Willy yelled. "Fuck you Larry, if you're going to shoot me, you're gonna have to look at me."

"Fine suit yourself." and without any hesitation fires two rounds into Willy's chest. The impact from the projectiles threw Willy backwards a good five feet, landing in an apparently lifeless heap.

The cold-blooded execution of Willy has caused Larry no more remorse then the killing of a pesky fly. Whistling tunelessly Larry spun on his heel, and walked back to the car, already visualizing his next steps. Speeding off in a cloud of dust, Larry would have been dumbfounded to see the apparently lifeless heap, begin to move.

Groaning, Willy slowly recovers from the impact of the two slugs hitting him in the chest at close range. With his hands still cuffed behind him, Willy has to roll onto his side then struggle to his knees. With what feels like a cracked sternum, these awkward movements cause severe pain, finally Willy can gain his feet. Standing with his feet spread apart to improve his balance, Willy realizes that if he takes shallow breaths the pain is not as severe. The fact that he is still alive, is thanks mainly to his constant reading of the Police personal protection magazine. Not wanting people to laugh at him because he's a cop in a small town, Willy was wearing the latest model bullet proof vest, which he had purchased for himself. With a wry smile, Willy now thinks the purchase was worth every penny.

As Jeb and TJ say their goodbyes and promise to stay in touch, Mike fervently wishes he had had the same opportunity to say goodbye to his girls.

As the trio climb into the car and take their leave, Jeb is almost overcome with longing as he already misses TJ. Hearing an impatient nicker from his horses Jeb remembers they are still saddled. Having removed the saddles and turned them into the corral, Jeb watches as they perform the ritual of rolling in the dirt. The snapping of a dry twig alerts Jeb to the fact there is someone else nearby.

BLURRED LINE

Not looking over his shoulder to identify the person, Jeb states. "I love you brother, but you're an idiot. That boy needs his dad. It's time you quit making excuses, and be the man I know you can be."

Moving to stand beside his brother, Clive acknowledges the truth in Jebs statement. "You're right I'm an idiot, and yes he needs his dad. I just hope that I can once again be that guy for TJ."

Clapping his brother on the shoulder Jeb declares. "Well fuckin hiding out here sure isn't proving anything!"

Smiling at his brother Clive asks him. "Why are you always right?"

"Smarter than you," Jeb replies simply.

As the vehicle with Irene, Mike and TJ heads towards town, they spot a figure walking down the middle of the road with hands clasped behind their back.

As Irene's car rapidly closes in on the pedestrian she murmurs. "Oh fuck!"

Stopping the car abreast of the pedestrian, Irene quickly exits the vehicle, Mike is right behind her.

With tears rolling down his cheeks Willy bawls out. "I fucked up Irene."

"What the fuck happened here Willy?" she demanded. "You were supposed to take Larry to jail."

As Willy relates what happened Irene is instantly contrite when she hears that Willy had been shot. Moving behind Willy, Mike releases the handcuffs. Willy is not cognizant of the fact his hands are released as he continues holding his arms behind his back until Mike gently pushes them forward.

Worried now for her friend's well-being Irene rips open Willy's shirt and reveals the bullet proof vest. Nestled in the very center of the vest are the two slugs that were meant to end Willy's life. Having now established that Willy is not likely going to succumb to his injuries, Irene is once again very angry.

BLURRED LINE

With a look of disgust, Mike states somewhat redundantly. "We're right back to square one," staring at Willy with a look of annoyance, mixed with frustration Mike tells him unequivocally that if he worked for Mike he would be suspended.

Jumping into the fray Irene advises Willy in a scathing tone of voice. "You are now suspended from active duty pending a hearing on your actions today!"

Re-joining TJ, who all this while has been patiently waiting in the vehicle, Irene engages the emergency lights and siren and speeds to town. Arriving back at the South- Bend Police station, Irene advises Mike that she will run Willy to the hospital.

She suggests that TJ, and Mike grab some supper at Nina's and hopefully she will be able to join them shortly.

Entering Nina's diner TJ insists they sit at the counter, amused by this Mike readily agrees. Watching TJ stare at the neatly placed glassware, Mike finally sees what TJ is looking at. Hidden among the neatly stacked glasses is a small mirror, TJ informs him that this is where Larry always sat, in order to see everyone coming in without turning around.

"Must be the wolf instinct," Mike spoke with a sardonic twist.

"What's that?" asked TJ

"Someone once said there are wolves and there are sheep."

Asking the waitress what the dinner special is, they both decide on the deluxe cheeseburger with fries. TJ then poses a question for Mike. "Now that Larry has escaped, will I still be able to go home?"

Staring at his half-eaten burger apparently lost in thought he finally looks up and informs TJ that right now Larry poses no threat. "Larry is not aware that Willy survived; but having said that, he is smart enough to know that when we discover that he is not here in jail there will be an all-points bulletin issued for his immediate arrest," explained Mike.

As Irene joins the two at the counter she apologizes for being so long.

BLURRED LINE

She explains that they will keep Willy overnight for
observation. She then suggests to them that since it is already
getting late why not follow her out to her place and they can stay
the night there.

Not looking forward to a long night of driving, Mike and TJ
readily agree, it takes only a few minutes and they arrive at a
spacious three-bedroom bungalow style home.

Upon entering the home, Mike and TJ were surprised by the
décor.

"I hope you guys like my interior decorating, this house was left
to me by my grand-mother and it was in a pretty bad state."
Staring at the decor Mike and TJ are speechless, realizing their
hostess might interpret their silence the wrong way, insist that it
is very contemporary.

After TJ, has told Mike and Irene all about himself and his
family, he finds it impossible to stifle a yawn.

"I'm sorry TJ," exclaimed Irene, you must be exhausted, I'll
show you your room.

Re-entering the kitchen Irene asks Mike if he would like a beer.
"Sounds good."

Handing Mike two glacial cold beers from the fridge, Irene
directs him into the living room telling him she will be right back
as she needs to change.

Settling onto the divan and using the wall as a back-rest Mike
can't help but whistle when Irene appears wearing a simple
flowered Caftan.

Settling herself down beside Mike she touches her bottle of
beer to Mike's in a silent toast, and takes a small sip. After a few
moments of companionable silence Irene remarks. "Please don't
be offended Mike, but Chance seems a rather different last name
for a man clearly of Asian descent."

Savoring the taste of the cold beer Mike responded.

BLURRED LINE

"No offense Irene, my grandfather emigrated here when he was a young man, he thought that if he Anglicized his last name integrating might be easier. His last name was Chang Yee, so he went with Chance."

As the evening progresses, Mike begins to relate to Irene what befell his family. She was shocked and outraged that Adele would blame him for the girl's disappearance.

"Do you think this Sergeant and his niece were responsible?"

"I really don't know," mused a thoughtful Mike. "I find it disturbing that neither one of them disclosed the fact they are related. If it weren't for my old lieutenant remembering that Ellen used to visit O'Mallory at the precinct, I still wouldn't be aware of the relationship. On the surface this revelation makes their actions somewhat questionable, but I have never given them a reason to hate me enough to take my children."

Glancing at the clock Irene is shocked to see how long they have been sitting there talking. Rising from the divan Irene silently extends an invitation to Mike by holding out her hand to him. Mike just as silently accepts the invitation, by gently grasping the hand and standing up.

CHAPTER TWENTY-SEVEN

Seated at the kitchen table the following morning, Mike and TJ have endured a breakfast prepared by Irene. There was half cooked bacon, fried eggs that were still so runny that had to be corralled with the burnt toast, else they would slide off the plate.

Declaring this to be one of the best breakfasts ever, Mike asked TJ if he is ready to hit the road.

"Ya. It will be nice to see my mom again," stated an exuberant TJ as he pushes away the remainder of his uneaten breakfast with a small grimace.

As they say their goodbyes TJ notices that Mike and Irene are staring at each other.

Having driven a couple of blocks away from Irene's, TJ begins to laugh.

"What's so funny?" queried Mike.

"It's a good thing Irene is a cop and not a decorator," exclaimed a laughing TJ.

Joining in with a small chuckle of his own Mike agreed with this. Then added dryly. "Her cooking ability is somewhat challenged also."

On a more serious note TJ asks Mike. "What makes a guy like Larry do the things he does. I mean he's a cop, he's supposed to protect people not hurt them".

Thinking about the best way to answer this Mike begins. "Well I'm certainly no psychologist TJ, but I think that at some point in their lives everyone will cross the line between right and wrong. Even you TJ, maybe you took a candy bar or pop that never belonged to you when you were younger.

BLURRED LINE

Thankfully for the sake of an orderly society, most people return to the right side of the line but, there are some that prefer the wrong side. They don't like the rules that govern society, the thin line between right and wrong becomes blurred and they are no longer able to differentiate between the two," appearing to warm up to this subject Mike continues. "What really pisses me off is when people like Larry, abuse the trust that is inherently accepted when you become a cop. They are now on the wrong side of that line and need to be stopped."

Thinking about what he was seeing at breakfast this morning TJ switches the subject and asks Mike. "Are you married?"

Able to discern the motive behind TJ's question Mike informs TJ that he isn't, his wife Adele had left him a while ago.

"Do you have kids?"

"I have the two most beautiful daughters you could ever imagine." replied a somber Mike.

"Do they live with your ex?"

"Tell you what TJ, it's long story and maybe someday I will tell you, but not right now."

Smarting from this mild rebuke TJ stares out the window at the passing landscape.

Having thought long and hard about whether to divulge to TJ about what he discovered before leaving for South bend Mike feels that he has no alternative. "TJ, before I left the city, I was advised that the person who is co-operating with the police, took them to a place where a body with a single gunshot wound to the head was found."

Looking intently at Mike, TJ wonders why he is telling him this. Then as he considers Mike words, it dawns on him that this must be the person whose murder he witnessed.

Seeing that he has TJ's undivided attention Mike drops a bomb. "Your best friends name is Benjamin Harris, right?"

Nodding in the affirmative, unable to speak TJ is terrified of where this is going.

BLURRED LINE

"I'm so sorry to have to tell you this TJ, but, the victim has been identified as Blake Harris, your friend's dad."

As TJ absorbs this information, he's immediately filled with self-loathing thinking that if he hadn't been so concerned for his own safety he might have been able to intervene.

Appearing to read TJ's thoughts Mike assures him that if TJ had tried to intervene, there would be two victims instead of one. Completely disconsolate, TJ lapses into a quiet reverie, staring out the window, but not seeing the passing scenery.

After a couple of short pit stops, TJ is dozing with his head uncomfortably wedged between the window and his seat when Mike softly calls his name.

"Hey TJ, you're home."

Opening his eyes TJ is greeted by all the familiar sights of home. Exiting the car, he sees his mom slowly making her way home from where the bus drops her off, running to meet her TJ picks her up and swings her around. Ophelia's eyes instantly fill with tears of happiness as she realizes her youngest son is home.

Pretending to be annoyed, she demands to be put down, as TJ obeys her wishes Ophelia bestows upon her son a hug that is reserved solely for mothers and their sons.

Mike has been watching this heartfelt reunion between TJ and his mom, and is happy that he's played a small part in it.

Holding his mom's hand TJ makes his way back to Mike, where Ophelia holds out her hand and fervently thanks Mike.

Taking his leave Mike heads to the empty apartment he calls home. Although it was incredible watching TJ and his mom, it has also driven home the fact that there is no one waiting to greet him.

Later that night with his feet resting on the tattered ottoman Mike finds himself thinking about Irene. He knows that he would like to see her again and perhaps they might be able to forge a relationship. Surprised at seeing his cell phone begin to vibrate its way across the small kitchen table Mike idly wonders who's calling this late.

BLURRED LINE

Smiling in anticipation when he discovers its Irene's number on caller display, Mike answers. After Irene inquired about their drive home she turns serious.

Advising Mike that she was issued a search warrant for Larry's residence and personal car. She admits they found nothing substantial in the house, but upon searching the car she discovered a small scrap of paper that had fallen under the front passenger seat.

"Michael, written on that scrap of paper were the names Alicia and Desiree. There is also written the names of what is obviously a married couples name, address and phone number."

At first Mike's heart skipped a couple of beats upon hearing Irene call him Michael. But hearing the rest of what she has said has Mike confused, why the hell would his daughter's names be on a scrap of paper in Larry's car. About to ask Irene the name of the couple, she advises Mike that she has located where these people reside. Thanking Irene profusely for this information Mike ends the call. Quickly donning his jacket, he is torn as to what this information might mean. *Why the fuck would Larry have my daughter's names associated with people who live three thousand miles away?*

CHAPTER TWENTY-EIGHT

Arriving in the early morning Mike exits the aircraft, and follows the signs directing all passengers to the arrivals area. Spotting his last name printed on a piece of cardboard Mike heads in that direction. Shaking the hand of the sign bearer Mike introduces himself, noting his greeter bears the permanently tanned face so common to this hot southern climate.

Introducing himself as Frank Hodgkin, he quickly brings Mike up to speed. The local Police Department has the address in question under surveillance, Mike and himself will head there right now. Frank states that the registered owners of this property are extremely affluent, they are also very private with little or no public exposure.

Listening to this with a grim countenance, Mike can only hope that he may soon be reunited with his daughters.

Bringing the patrol car to a slow halt in front of a what appears to be a mansion Frank looks at Mike and speaking sardonically remarks. "Told you so."

Proceeding up to the massive front door Mike feels his hands become slick with nervous sweat. Rapping loudly on the door, Frank then appears to take malicious enjoyment leaning on the doorbell.

Not quite knowing what to expect, Mike and Frank are not really surprised when the door is opened by an older gentleman, who speaks with what they surmise to be a British accent.

"Are you Mr. Bartholomew Jacobs?" brusquely demanded Frank.

"No I am not. My name is Wynn and I am the butler."

BLURRED LINE

With a wry grin directed at Mike, and expressive shrug of his shoulders Frank mutters. "Why am I not fuckin surprised." then he advises Wynn they would like to speak to Mr. or Mrs. Jacobs. "And what may I say is the nature of your business?"

Pointing to his detective shield Frank declares "Tell him he better talk to me or he's going for a ride."

As the door closes, Frank utters a heart-felt blasphemy concerning people who have too much wealth.

After a wait of about five minutes, the door is once again re-opened by Wynn and they are directed to follow him to the study.

Entering a spacious room with vaulted ceiling, and book shelves that line one complete wall they are met by a couple who regard Mike and Frank with a look of complete disdain.

Unable to restrain himself any longer Mike's large frame advances quickly towards the husband seated in a chair with his wife standing behind his shoulder.

"I want to know why my daughter's name was on the same piece of paper that yours was," demanded a fully enraged Mike.

"I resent the way you're addressing us," replied the husband in a falsetto voice.

Standing with his hands placed on his hips Mike is barely able to restrain himself from mimicking the husbands voice.

Mrs. Jacobs now advises Mike that they wish their attorney to be present.

"That's fine you call him, but in the meantime, I will ask you again why your name appears with my daughter's name on a piece of paper located in a known felon's vehicle."

During this confrontation, Frank, has noticed what he takes to be a maid looking at him, then nervously looking away.

Knowing that the Jacobs will not relinquish anything useful unless it serves their purpose, Frank goes in search of the maid.

He doesn't have far to go, leaving the study he just rounds a corner and sees her pointing to a closed door.

BLURRED LINE

Assuming she wants him to enter, Frank finds himself in a smaller room full of cleaning agents. With a quick furtive look over her shoulder the maid enters shortly behind Frank.
"Senor, is it two young girls you seek?" whispered the maid
"Yes, it is, what do you know about these girls?"
"Senor, they have been here for seven months."
"Where are they?" demanded Frank
"They left three nights back," whimpered the maid
Raising his voice above a stage whisper, Frank now demands that she tell him all she knows.
"One night about seven months ago, these two young girls Desiree and Alicia arrived here. They were so beautiful, the master said they adopted them but we knew better. The master thinks we are furniture and speaks as though we don't hear. I overheard the Master say that twenty thousand per kid was too much, the Mistress told him to pay it if he wanted her to stay with him. We were instructed to tell the girls their parents had died in a car crash, and now the Master and Mistress were their new parents. The younger one would not stop crying, she wanted her mommy and daddy. The older one was very brave she would get angry at the masters. Finally, the Mistress. said she could no longer tolerate the crying brat and wanted them gone." taking a deep breath, she continued. "It was late at night when a car showed up, I was told to get the girls dressed and out to the car with all their belongings. There was a man and woman in the car, I think they knew the girls as they called them by name, they took the girls, and the master warned us not to speak of them again."
Appalled by what he is hearing Frank instructs the frightened girl to stay put. Striding quickly back to the study he orders the Jacobs to stay put, and tells Mike that he needs to come with him.
Once again in the room with the maid, Frank asks her what her name is.
"Celia," she quavered.

BLURRED LINE

"Tell him exactly what you told me," ordered Frank.
As the story is once again related to Mike, he is shaken to his
core by what he hears.

When Celia reaches the point about the man and the woman in
the car, Mike holds up his hand and directs her to stop. Deciding
to play a hunch concerning the missing O'Mallory and Ellen.

Mike retrieves his phone from his pocket and quickly accesses
the Metro-City Police Department, pulling up O'Mallory's
picture he shows it to Celia asking if this is the man.

Her wide eyes are all the answer they need, sobbing she asks
them what will happen to her. She needs this job as her parents
back home depend on the money she sends to them.
With a look of disgust, Mike tells her he hopes she gets deported,
or failing that she goes to jail for aiding and abetting.

Mike left the small room, and raced back to the study, walked
up to Jacobs, and with one hand lifts him bodily out of the chair.
"Who the fuck do you people think you are? You buy and sell
kids like a fuckin commodity!" roared Mike
"You can't talk to me like that!" squealed an indignant Jacobs.
"You stupid son of a bitch, you don't realize that right now you
are a hairs breath away from a beating that will likely kill you."
bellowed an out of control Mike.
Whining in abject fear Jacobs pleads with Frank to stop this
madman.
"Fuck you Jacobs," growled an equally enraged Frank. "Right
now, we're not cops, we're fathers."

"What chance did you give my little girls, did you take pity on
them and attempt to contact their parents and end their
nightmare. No, you didn't, you sack of shit," having said that,
the pent-up emotions of the previous eight months were
unleashed in a sudden flurry of blows to the head and body of
Jacobs. The sound of his jaw breaking, was clearly audible to
everyone in the room, the now unconscious Jacobs fell
unceremoniously to the floor. Stepping back, Mike glared in
disgust at the unmoving form of Jacobs.

BLURRED LINE

"Well now look at that," declared Frank with a menacing look at Jacobs wife as if daring her to contradict him. "That clumsy son of a bitch tripped over his own two feet and knocked himself out when he hit the floor," casually looking at the inert form adds. "Stupid fuck probably broke his jaw too."

At this point in time, Frank places a call to the other cops waiting outside, to enter the premises and take everyone on the property into custody for questioning.
As Mike and Frank watch the parade of servants walk by in cuffs, Mike unleashes a torrent of hatred for these people.

Slamming a fist repeatedly onto the hood of Frank's car, completely disgusted with these people Mike growls. "What the fuck? Are we back in the days of slaves? People are being bought and sold like a fuckin commodity."
"Unfortunately, Mike it's people like these Jacobs that are the real problem. They have the financial resources to circumvent normal procedures, if there are no buyers there can't be any sellers. I realize it's small comfort Mike but, I will do my best to see they face the full brunt of the law regarding their actions!"

Feeling utterly devastated that he has missed his daughters by a lousy seventy-two hours, he feels himself begin to spiral downwards into a despair filled abyss. He decides to call the one person he feels connected to. Before the connection is made Frank appears before him with the Butler in tow, canceling the call Mike looks at Frank and asks. "What's up?"

Pointing at the butler Frank states. "This sack of shit has something he wants to tell you."
"For what it's worth, you have two incredible daughters. I felt that my employer was involved in something that is morally corrupt, I therefore took the liberty of noting the license plate number as well as the make and model of the vehicle that came to collect the girls. If you reach into my vest pocket, you will find the information written down."

BLURRED LINE

Following Wynn's directions Mike locates the paper, and Frank, even though O'Mallory has a seventy-two-hour head start initiates the newly created Amber Alert child rescue program.

As Frank begins leading Wynn away to the waiting cars, Mike yells at him. "Hey asshole, where's the accent?"
Turning to look at Mike and answering in a stoical tone of voice. "It's as phony as I am," adding. "I apologize to you sir, for

not having the courage to do what was right," and with that turns and walks towards a future that will hopefully include time spent in prison.

Turning away in disgust at what humanity has apparently become, Mike is about to call Irene when he feels his phone vibrate. Wondering who the unknown number is Mike answers his phone, he is not prepared for who the caller is.

"Hey buddy how you doing?" all these cops here remind me of flies on a carcass. Well you have screwed this up royally, I was going to put the touch on these rich assholes. They seem to have paid everyone else except yours truly."

Not comprehending what Larry is saying, Mike asks. "What the fuck are you talking about asshole?"

"Well it seems that O'Mallory and the Delveccio's with the cooperation of Ellen put this whole thing together. The only problem is they forgot to include yours truly. So, I thought I would just inform these kind people that they forgot to pay me as well."

Aghast at this revelation, Mike is barely able to speak. "What the fuck?" what did I ever do to them?" then in disbelief adds. "Larry, for fucks sake you're Desiree's godfather!"

"Answering your question buddy, I hear O'Mallory didn't like your attitude."

"How can you do this? You fuckin asshole! If I ever see you again I will unleash a world of hurt on you that will have you begging for a grave."
"Nothing personal buddy, it's all about the money. Say, those rich bastards sure have a lot of servants don't they."

BLURRED LINE

Becoming cognizant of what Larry is saying, Mike slowly begins to revolve his head searching for Larry.

Laughing harshly Larry taunts Mike. "That's right buddy turn your head maybe you see me, maybe you don't, but I certainly see you."

Noticing a tanned bald head on the periphery of the crowd, turned away and clearly talking on a cell phone, Mike begins to stalk his quarry. Silently walking on the balls of his feet Mike quickly closes the gap, his hand is on the butt of his weapon ready to draw it when his quarry turns to face him. Nodding at Mike, the local detective moves away while continuing his conversation.

"Hey that was fun to watch buddy, but I better get going, too many cops around here," stated Larry accompanied by a maniacal laugh.

Jesus Christ, Mike swears to himself. If I ever see that fucker again I will fuckin shoot first and ask questions later.

Staring at his phone, Mike almost drops it when it begins to vibrate in his hand. Seeing who the caller is Mike answers it, in a voice that clearly conveys the utter devastation he is feeling, he informs Irene that he missed his daughters by a lousy three fuckin days.

"That is terrible news Michael," sympathized Irene. "I can't leave here right now for obvious reasons, so why don't you come home to South -Bend and together we will figure out how to find your daughters."

BLURRED LINE

.

Author's note. Watch for the exciting conclusion coming in early 2017.

Robert Lane

Made in the USA
Middletown, DE
08 April 2017